THE KNIGHTLY QUEST

OTHER BOOKS BY TENNESSEE WILLIAMS

Novel

The Roman Spring of Mrs. Stone

Plays

Cat on a Hot Tin Roof
The Eccentricities of a Nightingale & Summer and Smoke
The Glass Menagerie
The Milk Train Doesn't Stop Here Anymore
The Night of the Iguana
Orpheus Descending
Period of Adjustment
A Streetcar Named Desire
Suddenly Last Summer
Three Plays: Camino Real
           The Rose Tattoo
           Sweet Bird of Youth
27 Wagons Full of Cotton

Poetry

In the Winter of Cities

Screenplay

Baby Doll

Stories

Hard Candy
One Arm

TENNESSEE WILLIAMS

THE KNIGHTLY QUEST

A NOVELLA
AND FOUR SHORT STORIES

A NEW DIRECTIONS BOOK

CONTENTS

THE KNIGHTLY QUEST

THE KNIGHTLY

QUEST

W HEN Gewinner Pearce returned home after
years of travel with a tutor-companion, the late Dr.
Horace Greaves, everything visible from the airport,
including the airport itself, was so unrecognizable to
him that he thought the plane must have made an un-
scheduled stop. He was about to hurry back up the
steps to the plane's cabin when he heard the voice of a
woman calling his name. He gazed out toward the di-
rection from which the call issued and what he saw
was a young woman approaching him with the ve-
locity of a football tackler and with a mink coat flapping about her. For a couple of moments she was in-
tercepted and restrained in her approach by a pair of
armed guards.

I

Hands off, hands off me! Don't you know who I am? I am Mrs. Braden Pearce, out here to meet the brother of my husband! His name's Gewinner—the same as the name of the town.

The steel-helmeted guards fell back from her with awkward little deferential salutes, and then she continued her rush toward Gewinner, who defended and braced himself as best he could by placing vertically before him his furled black silk umbrella and tensing his slight body to withstand the moment of impact. But he was surprised and relieved that this young wife of his brother, never seen before, slackened her pace just before she reached him, and instead of colliding with him, she introduced herself to him in a manner that was fast and vigorous but reasonably coherent.

Oh, Gewinner, she cried out to him as if he were in a far corner of the airfield, I bet you don't know who I am, I am Braden's wife, Violet, and Mother Pearce, God love her, was dying to meet you herself but she just couldn't make it because today is the day she's placing a wreath on the memorial to our boys in Kwat Sing How, and so, God love her, she appointed me in her place to welcome you home here.

Oh. Good, said Gewinner.

They were now moving toward the airport building, Violet still holding up her end of the unilateral conversation. How was your flight, was it nice? I recognized you the moment you started down the steps from the plane, not because you look like your brother, Braden, you don't a bit in the world, but you did look exactly like the way I expected you to look, I swear you did, and you do!

How did you expect me to look? asked Gewinner with unaffected interest in what her answer might be. He had a touch of the Narcissan in his nature and was always somewhat curious about the way he might appear to persons unaccustomed to his appearance.

Why, I know the family called you Prince, they did and still do, and if anybody ever looked like a prince out of a fairy-tale book, it's you, God love you, you do!

Then, without pause, she cried out, Oh, my God, they're playing "Babe's Stomp" again!

Playing what? asked Gewinner.

Babe, Babe, Babe, the President's daughter, you know!

No, I don't know, said Gewinner.

Well, first there was "Babe's Hop," and now there's "Babe's Stomp," and I want you to know that as much as I detested the hop, this stomp of hers makes the hop seem like a lovely thing to look back on, it actually does, no fooling!

Violet was referring to rhythm-band music that was coming thunderously from a sound apparatus atop the terminal building. It made the airport sound like a big discothèque, and several incoming passengers and persons there to receive them were going into spastic, stamping gyrations.

Gewinner shouted over this hullaballoo:

3

What's wrong with the air? he shouted; it has a peculiar smell to it.

Oh, that, shouted Violet, that's just the fumes from The Project.

What's The Project? Gewinner shouted back at her.

Shouting was unnecessary now, for "Babe's Stomp" had quit as abruptly as it had started. Gewinner's shouted question drew undesired attention in the sudden, comparative silence. People glanced at him with expressions of curiosity or incredulity or both.

Out of the side of her mouth, Violet said, No talk about it right now.

Then she called out the name William, William!

A dead-pan, uniformed man, presumably employed by the family, emerged from the airport crowd to take Gewinner's baggage-claim checks.

Now then, said Violet, we'll go wait in the car and get acquainted, unless you could use a wee drink at the bar. Frankly, I hope you can. I could sure in hell use a stinger under my belt. Whenever I rush about, it makes me thirsty. So come along, Prince, right up these steps here, to the Sky-lite Lounge. You know, we're all so excited that you've come home from your travels. Let's sit at the bar, it's quicker. Now where were you last in your travels?

In the Land of the Midnight Sun, said Gewinner, knowing from the wild but glazed look in her eyes that she'd pay no attention to this answer, which was made up. Where he'd last been in his travels was actually in Manhattan where his tutor-companion, Dr.

4

Greaves, had fallen fatally prey to an overdosage of a drug he'd taken to expand his perceptions. This drug had not only expanded the perceptions of Dr. Greaves but had deranged them somewhat, so that the good, gray philosopher and doctor of humanities had walked right off the roof of a five-story brownstone in the Turtle Bay section of Manhattan as if he were responding to a call from outer space, which may have been exactly what he was doing. . . .

In the cocktail lounge of the airport, Gewinner asked for a campari and soda but didn't get it, the drink being unknown to the barman. Violet showed a somewhat assertive streak in her nature by telling the barman to give them both stingers. She tossed down hers as fast as if she were putting out a fire in her stomach, and then she said to Gewinner, Why, Prince, you didn't drink enough of that stinger to keep a bird alive! Oh well, I'll finish it for you. So she tossed down Gewinner's stinger too. Now then, she said, that's what the doctor ordered and I obeyed the order, so let's make a run for the car before the family fink suspects we've been up here, Gewinner.

In the car on the way home, if home you could call it, Gewinner continued to observe almost nothing he had once known in the town which had now grown to a city. The sylvan park whose trees had been mostly willows had turned into a concrete playground full of monkeys disguised as children, at least that was the impression made upon Gewinner.

To himself more than to Violet he observed, I remember it being like a romantic ballet setting. I mean swans drifted about on a lake and there were cranes, herons, flamingos and even a peacock with several peahens around him, but now there's not a willow and not a swan or a lake for a swan to drift in.

Aw now, said Violet, you mustn't philosophize gloomily about it.

I wasn't philosophizing, I was simply remembering and observing, said Gewinner.

He gave Violet a rather sharp glance, wondering where she had gotten her education, if any.

I reckon you don't realize it, said Violet, pressing his arm as if to comfort him, but all these changes you notice are because of The Project.

And what exactly is that? asked Gewinner again.

Prince, you're not serious, are you!

Perfectly. I've never heard of The Project.

Well, now you have, said Violet, and furthermore you're just about to see it, the outside of it! There! Here! Look at it!

The limousine was now going by what appeared to be an enormous penitentiary for criminals of the most dangerous nature. Its grounds were enclosed by a tall metal fence on which, at intervals, were signs that said DANGER, ELECTRICALLY CHARGED, and just inside this enclosure, patrolling the grounds, were uniformed men with dogs. The dogs seemed to want to go faster than the men, they kept tugging at their leads and glancing back crossly at the men. Then the dogs would look ahead again with expressions that could

6

be described as fiercely glaring. The men's and dogs' heads would pivot slightly from right to left and left to right as if the men and dogs had gone to the same training school and come out equally proficient at the art of patrolling, and it would be hard to say, if you had to, which glared more fiercely, the human guards or the dogs.

Why, here, said Gewinner, almost exclaiming about it, was my father's business, the Red Devil Battery Plant.

Yes, isn't it wonderful? said Violet with a certain sibilance in her speech. Your father's, God love your father, his Red Devil Battery Plant has been converted into The Project, and I want you to know that your brother, Braden Pearce, is the top man on the totem pole here, and it's not just great, it's the greatest!

What does The Project make or do? asked Gewinner.

Oh, I do love you, Prince, cried out Violet. To think you honestly don't know what The Project is for! Why, Prince, it's for the development of a thing to blow them all off the map of the world, for good and all and forever!

Who is them?

Why, *them* is *them,* who else! Are you serious, Prince, or are you just putting me on about it?

He heard a quick scratching sound and saw that she had snatched a little appointment book from her purse and was scribbling down something. She tore the page out and pressed it into his hand.

7

The message was: Change the subject, I think this car is bugged.

Gewinner had hardly read this peculiar message when Violet snatched the paper back from him, crumpled it, thrust it into her mouth, ground it between her teeth, swallowed, gagged, coughed, pressed a button that turned the radio on, clutched her throat and swallowed again, this time successfully.

Immediately after this curious series of actions, or compulsive syndrome, she began to chatter again.

Prince? Gewinner? I wish you could have seen the delighted expressions on their faces, Mama's and Braden's, when they heard you were on your way back here all of a sudden! It was a sight to behold, that I can tell you. Oh, here we are! Recognize it?

The car had turned into the drive of a gray stone building that had a resemblance, probably more deliberate than accidental, to something in the nature of an ancient Saracen castle brought up to date.

It's all that I've recognized since I got off the plane, said Gewinner, telling almost the truth.

Without asking questions, just by listening to and piecing together scraps of conversation, Gewinner came to know, in the following days, a number of things that accounted for the town's changes, such as the fact that his late father's Red Devil Battery Plant had sure enough been converted into a thing called The Project, and that The Project was engaged all day and all night in the development of some marvel-

8

ously mysterious weapon of annihilation. The number of its personnel was greater than had been the town's population at the time when Gewinner had set out on his travels. Hordes of scientists, technicians, brass hats of degree high and low, intelligence officers, highly skilled workmen and ordinary workmen, all the way up and down the totem pole of importance, were involved in The Project's operations. As Violet put it, it was not only great but the greatest, not a bit of exaggeration about it.

The Project's personnel and their families were housed in new little concrete-block structures called Sunshine Houses, and a lot of new businesses, big and little, had sprung up to accommodate their needs and wholesome pleasures, most of them also named something very cheerful such as "Sweetheart," "Rainbow" and "Blue Bird."

One of these new businesses, between big and little, was the Laughing Boy Drive-in, situated on a corner diagonally across from the Pearce family mansion, and this drive-in provoked Gewinner Pearce's sense of personal outrage more strongly than any other vulgarity which had appeared in his home town during his absence. The drive-in was built on property that belonged to the Pearces. Gewinner's younger brother, Braden, had leased it for ninety-nine years to a boyhood chum whose portrait in golden neon smiled and laughed out loud with a big haw-haw, at ten-second intervals, from early dusk till midnight. And this, mind you, was on the finest residential boulevard in

9

the city and the haw-hawing neon portrait of its
owner was almost directly facing the Pearce mansion.
Gewinner, of course, had no misapprehensions about
the elegance and dignity of the Pearce place, but the
fact remained that Gewinner was a Pearce, and the
Laughing Boy in neon seemed a personal affront. It
laughed so loudly that it punctuated all but the loud-
est passages of the symphonic music he played on his
hi-fi at night to calm his nerves, and in addition to the
haw-haw at the drive-in there was the honking of cars
from morn to midnight, appealing for immediate serv-
ings of such items as King-burgers, barbecued ribs,
malts, cokes, coffee and so forth. The carhops were
girls and sometimes they'd lose control of their nerves
under the constant pressure of their jobs and would
have screaming fits; then, more than likely, there'd be
the siren wail of an ambulance or a squad car or both.
When the hysterical carhop had been rushed off to the
Sunshine Emergency Center, the Laughing Boy
would seem to be splitting his sides over the whole
bit, and though Gewinner could understand how it
all might seem ludicrous, in a ghastly way, the me-
chanical haw-haw somehow would kill the joke, at
least for the prince of the Pearces.

Now for a little digression in the nature of turning
back time.

While Gewinner had been on his travels he received
from his mother exactly two communications a year, a
cablegram at Christmas and a cablegram at Easter,
both addressed to him care of American Express in

London, a capital that Gewinner visited from time to time to refurbish his wardrobe. These cablegrams were very much to the point. The Christmas one said, Christ is born, Love, Mother, and the Easter one said, Christ is risen, Love, Mother. And once, between Christmas and Easter, Gewinner dispatched a cablegram to Mother Pearce that was utterly meaningless to her: it said, Dear Mother, What is He up to now? Love, Gewinner.

However, actually Mother Pearce's correspondence was far and away more loquacious than these twice yearly announcements to her traveling son would suggest, and "loquacious" is the *mot juste* for it, since all her outgoing letters and wires were shouted to a personal secretary, little Miss Genevieve Goodleigh. And "shouted" is the correct way to put it, as this correspondence was dictated while Mother Pearce was receiving her Vibra-Wonder treatment, a very loud, three-hour treatment that kept her from looking her age by a comfortable margin of give or take a few hours.

Now on this particular morning to which time has been reversed, a wire had come in from Gewinner, but Mother Pearce ignored all incoming letters and messages till after she'd shouted out, to the phenomenal Miss Goodleigh, her outgoing correspondence, and "phenomenal" is the precise term for Miss Goodleigh since she caught every word of this correspondence even when the Vibra-Wonder was operating in the highest of its five gears.

At this time, on this particular morning, Mother

Pearce was shouting out a letter to the most prominent hostess in the nation's capital.

Darling Boo, she shouted, I am telling you no news that is news to you when I tell you the President and the First Lady with their divine daughter, Babe, were house guests of mine last weekend, and, oh my soul and body, what fun we girls had together while the menfolks were holding their top-level consultations on the crisis in Ghu-Ghok-Shu. Of course I already knew from previous get-togethers that the First Lady is more fun than a barrel or a boatload of monkeys, but this last visit was one continual howl. The climax of it was a jamboree at the Club Diamond Brite. I said to Mag, The ship of state is in responsible hands so we don't have to worry about it, and I want you to know we didn't, why, honey, while the Chief and my precious boy Braden were deciding where to strike next and what to strike with, you would never have guessed from our fun and frolic that anything more serious than a possum hunt was going on anywhere in the world. We had a couple of jazz bands to spell each other, we had the Wildcat Five which you know are the latest craze, we had a nigger you threw baseballs at and if you hit him he fell in a tank of cold water, and we had a couple of boxing kangaroos with a dog referee. So! What suddenly happened but this! The doors bang open at the height of the frolic and in comes my precious boy Braden pushing the Chief in a red, white and blue wheelbarrow, the Chief firing blanks out of two pistols. They were like two kids

who have just burnt down the schoolhouse, and I tell
you, honey, the photographers and newspaper boys
had a field day, they went absolutely hog-wild, and
the commotion and pandemonium was way, way out
of control till all of a sudden the band struck up
"Babe's Stomp," in honor of Babe, and Babe shot like
a cannonball over to my boy Braden and caught him
in such a bear hug that I was scared for a second she'd
crack his ribs. Do my stomp with me, honey, I heard
her holler, and off they stomped together. It was a
sight to be seen when they accidentally stomped into
the honorary co-hostess and knocked her into the pastry end of the buffet table. Then Babe hollered to the
band to play a slow number called "The Clinch," and,
well, you know, Boo, I don't embarrass easy and it
would be hard to find a First Lady as up-to-date as
Mag is. This is what Mag said to me, Boo, she leaned
over to me and said, Do you see what I see, Nelly?
Our two children are dancing so tight together you
couldn't paste a postage stamp between them, and
look at the look in their eyes, I could cry like I do at a
wedding!

Now what do you make of that, Boo? I'm sure you
must see the tragic irony of it. Poor Violet was never
and never could be cut out for her present position in
life, I mean she was suddenly escalated way up beyond her natural limitations and would be a happier
girl if she had recognized and never overstepped her
personal potential. However, what I feel, Boo, is that
here is a tragedy that can still be corrected in life. If

Braden and Babe have been drawn together by such a powerful attraction to each other and a little propinquity like this, I think it's the will of God and we ought to feel morally obliged to do everything we can to bring them together more often. I'm writing you this because you're in a perfect position to throw them together up there and I can throw them together down here, and believe you me, it would be much harder to hold Babe and Braden apart than it is to get them together. Boo, do you see my point? I know that question is unnecessary because if you don't see my point you'd have to be blind as ten bats in a belfry, which isn't the case with you, Boo. Your vision and your thinking apparatus have always been up to snuff and a good deal higher. I think just a bit more propinquity at banquets up there and at cookouts and frolics down here will salvage the lives of a pair of fine young people that providence meant for each other. Now, Boo, keep this under your hat but if you think my suggestion is as wonderful as I do, get back to me on the teletype right away with one word, "wonderful," but if you have any reservations or questions about it, get back to me with the word "fog," and—

Oh, cried out Miss Goodleigh, my pencil point's broke!

Well hell, exclaimed Mother Pearce, what's going on here this morning?

Having never heard her employer speak with such violence before, Miss Goodleigh rushed sobbing into the bathroom to pull herself together.

While she was in there, Mother Pearce completed her Vibra-Wonder treatment and, having nothing else to do at the moment, idly picked up a wire which had come in that morning. This wire happened to be from Gewinner. It went as follows: Dear Mother, I was shocked and sorry to hear that father has gone to his heavenly mansion. I feel that I ought to be with you in this time of grief and remain as long as necessary to straighten out the unexpected curtailment of my travel expenses. Kill no fatted calf but expect my homecoming within the next few days. Will wire the precise time later. Fondest love, Gewinner.

God have mercy upon us, cried out Mother Pearce. She had observed that the wire contained no phone number she could call, no address to which she could wire to let the Prince know how little she needed his presence to console her in her newly widowed condition.

Now to turn back time more than a little bit further, Gewinner had been on the go since the spring of his sixteenth year, since a morning in that spring when his tutor-companion, the late Dr. Horace Greaves, had convinced Father and Mother Pearce so quickly and easily that their first-born son, the Prince in the tower, could be better instructed in the humanities while traveling here and there among foreign lands and seas. The late Dr. Horace Greaves had hardly begun to address the parents on this topic when the late Mr. Pearce had boomed out, *Fine, wonderful, great, for God's sake get going,* and Mother Pearce had almost simultaneously buzzed the chauffeur to whisk her son and his tutor as fast as a streak of blue lightning out to the airport and not let them out of his sight till they'd boarded a plane and the plane was off the ground.

So began the travels of Gewinner with his tutor-companion.

Gewinner thrived on these travels but the tutor-companion developed a nervous condition, complicated by insomnia, which culminated in a collapse that was followed by several relapses, and he finally wound up in a Bavarian spa that specialized in the ice cure for nervous disorders. So poor Dr. Greaves was packed in ice for three months, his temperature kept at the temperature level of the fish and the lizard, and during that chilly period in the doctor's stoical experience on earth, Gewinner somehow managed to enlist in the navy. His hitch in the navy was remarkably short, it lasted for just ten days, give or take a few minutes. Then Gewinner was returned to civilian status and his name and all else pertinent to him was expunged from all records of the naval branch of the armed services, as if he, Gewinner, had never so much as existed.

Gewinner then wired Dr. Greaves: Get off the ice and let's get cracking again. And it just so happened that Dr. Greaves had, that very day the wire reached him, been taken out of the ice, and though the distinguished scholar and educator in the humanities had not yet had time to completely thaw out, he was at least as eager as Gewinner to get cracking again, especially toward the equator.

Two things occurred in close sequence to delay the resumption of their travels, and this delay was really more in the nature of a cancellation. One of these occurrences has been mentioned already, the fatal misadventure of Dr. Greaves in the Turtle Bay section of Manhattan, ironically at a farewell banquet on the roof of a five-story town house, a banquet at which the main course and the only course was a species of fungus related to the mushroom, under the influence of which the good doctor took off like a parachute jumper and ended his earthly travels on the inexorable pavement below. However, the second occurrence has yet to be mentioned. It was a bit of information that Gewinner received from a bank official, the information that his father had recently been planted in the family plot and that the estate had passed into the custody of Mother Pearce and the younger son, Braden. This circumstance affected Gewinner gravely, since it meant that his remittances would no longer be adequate to support his former high style of life and travel here and there on the earth's surface.

Gewinner suspected, sensibly, that if he went home for a while, it might not take him too long to convince Mother Pearce and his brother that he, Gewinner, had better be allowed to go on with his travels in the opulent style to which he was accustomed.

Though Gewinner's brother was a year younger than Gewinner, Braden Pearce had the maturity of a

family man while Gewinner kept about him a graceful, adolescent look, thanks to his slimness and the
quality of his skin, so smooth that it seemed to be
made without pores, the way that the finest silk shows
no sign of being woven.

Gewinner stayed in the tower of the gray stone
mansion which had been designed to have a sort of
pop-art resemblance to a medieval castle. He had
moved into the tower while he was in his early teens
in order to remove himself as far from the Pearce family life as the geography of the mansion permitted,
and he had had an iron fire escape, almost as steep as a
stepladder, put up between the lawn and a window of
the tower so that his restless comings and goings at
night would not disturb the family. They had called
him the Prince as much in awe as in mockery of his
refinements.

Braden Pearce had the look that football players get
when they have been in business and married for several years: coarsening, thickening, getting flushed in
the face, turning into one of those bullish men who
shatter all opposition by the sheer weight and energy
of their drive until drink softens them up at forty-five
or fifty and the heart quits on them at sixty.

Right now Braden was at the peak of his male
power. His wife, Violet, had a pale, dampish look in
the mornings as if she had spent the night in a steam
bath. Their bedroom, unfortunately for Gewinner,
was directly under his room in the tower and they
made noises like beasts of the jungle when they had

sex, which was about every night. At his climax, Braden would howl and curse, and at hers, Violet would cry out like a yard full of peacocks. Apparently they would also roll and thrash about in their ecstasies, knocking things off their bedside tables. Some nights Mrs. Pearce would come to their door and call out, Is something wrong in there? Son, Violet, is something wrong in there? Neither would answer at once. Violet would be sobbing and making sounds as if she were dying of strangulation and Braden would be cursing and huffing for a minute or so after Mother Pearce's anxious call at the door. Then, at last, they both would answer together in hoarse voices, No, no, Mother, no, Mother, everything's fine, go on back to bed, Mother.

One night a widowed lady and her bachelor son, the Fishers, residents of the house next door, came over for a bridge game that went on after Violet and Braden had gone up to bed. Gewinner was in the game because he loved to outwit his mother at bridge, and they were playing away when the howling, cursing and religious and profane exclamations began to reverberate through the castle. Mrs. Pearce kept clearing her throat and then she asked Gewinner to turn the hi-fi on, but Gewinner, grinning wickedly, said, Oh Mother, I can't concentrate on my game with music playing. I think, said Mrs. Pearce—but she never completed the statement, for just then some very heavy object, probably Braden, fell to the floor and there was a shower of plaster from the ceiling over the bridge game and the chandelier swung like a pendulum, to exaggerate only slightly. The neighbor lady, Gewinner's partner in the bridge game, made repeated coughing sounds, explaining that she had a frog in her throat, while brushing plaster dust off her clothes.

Hmmm, said Mrs. Pearce with a tight-lipped attempt at a smile, partner, I have to pass.

Then, being dummy, she got up from the table, murmuring, Excuse me a moment, and went clattering upstairs to knock at the young couple's door.

Son? Violet? she could be heard calling, and before she could ask if anything was wrong, Braden's voice boomed through the house, bellowing out, For Chrissake, will you keep your ass on the bed? And Violet cried out shrilly, You're killing me, honey, I'm dying, let's stay on the floor!

Mrs. Pearce's partner, a nervous bachelor in his late forties, was quite flurried and flushed, since scenes of this nature are particularly embarrassing to Southern boys in the presence of their mothers. He forgot what was trumps, he almost seemed to be putting down cards at random. Nobody said anything after the neighbor lady's announcement that she had a frog in her throat but she and her son took turns at coughing. Then Gewinner began talking out loud but as if to himself, selecting a subject that seemed to have no relevance to the games upstairs and down. The speech unwound itself evenly from his lips which wore a smile like Hamlet's or the Mona Lisa's, or rather a bit on the sly side and also a bit on the side of the quietly savage. What he said in this curiously elliptical mono-logue, under the swaying chandelier and the continu-ing shower of dust, would never pass the scrutiny of a logician, if it were put on paper—where it is now being put, as if it came from a tape recorder that had picked up the very free associations of a hallucinated romantic.

Mrs. Fisher, he said, as if he were talking to her, the course of history changed when a troop of mercenary foot soldiers, equipped with a new weapon called the long bow, plopped to their knees among the little wildflowers that sprinkled the morning-dew-spangled grass on a certain field, in Normandy I believe, which became known to history as the Field of Agin-court. . . .

Mama, was the bid five spades?

No, son, it was six diamonds, doubled and redou-bled, before the—

Oh.

Gewinner went on serenely and illogically as he played a brilliant game. Yes, he went on, the common foot soldiers didn't pick the wild flowers, probably didn't notice the wildflowers there, but set their ar-rows to the strings of their bows and let them fly at a charge of plumed knights in armor, and then some-thing snapped in the clear morning air and was going to stay snapped for the rest of human time. The long-bows' arrows struck with appalling accuracy, the charge of the knights was routed, the mercenary foot soldiers rose from the dew-sparkling field, rushed forward and knelt again upon the little wildflowers and let their arrows go twanging again at the white and silver foe on the field at Agincourt. I suppose it was a little bit like suddenly switching from a game of chess to a game of checkers. I mean the big game of sides against each other in the world. Am I making any sense? I doubt it. But since you're not listening to me, it doesn't make much difference. I used to feel that there was a sort of demented romanticism in this house being designed to suggest a medieval castle, but the absurdity went too far with the construction of the Laughing Boy Drive-in, catty-cornered across from the fake castle. The last time I was home for a visit, the castle had a banner flying from its tower, a bifurcated triangle of white silk emblazoned with a coat of arms and a motto, *Carpe Diem,* which means seize the day. All of which makes me suspect that back of the sun and way deep under our feet, at the earth's center, are not a couple of noble mysteries but a couple of joke books. However, as for myself, I still go out alone at night, and feel something back of the visible stars and something deep under my feet. I don't know what it is. Maybe it's just the pleasure of getting a little away from the fake medieval castle and the Laughing Boy Drive-in.

Pardon me, said Mrs. Fisher, did you say something?

I was just saying, said Gewinner, that every time the earth turns on its axis, a clerk in heaven, some badly paid little clerk, jots down another minus sign after whatever symbol they use for the Quixote syndrome, or whatever the hell they call it in heaven, and I don't know whether the angels burst into weeping or song every time.

The neighbor's son spoke up and said, What were you saying, Gewinner? I didn't catch it, either.

Oh, I was making no more sense than an agnostic priest mumbling Mass, but someone had to say something, and so I said that across the street, diagonally across from Pearce's Folly, there is a perfect little gem of neo-Colonial architecture that's famous for its barbecued ribs and chicken-in-a-basket and chocolate malts as thick as fresh cement and piping-hot everfresh coffee. And I'm not a liar when I tell you it makes as much noise, well, nearly as much, as Violet and Braden in bed, at least it's that noisy, or nearly, when one shift at The Project has sallied forth to make way for the next shift, let's see now, doubled, redoubled and you've lost seven tricks, what a blow for Mama when she comes back down.

The thumping on the floor above was still going on, and the son and mother, the Fishers, had turned from rose red to paper white, but the Widow Fisher produced her voice to ask Gewinner again what he was saying while she'd been preoccupied with her cards.

Oh, just babbling, he said, just to hear myself babbling, it helps my concentration to babble away playing cards. But when Mother Pearce comes down from her luckless effort to clip the wings of Eros, I'm going to make a suggestion, I'm going to suggest to her that she install a pipe organ in Violet's and Braden's bedroom behind a screen or tapestry. The organist could come in by way of a secret staircase and a sliding panel, and whenever Violet and Braden retire before guests have left the castle, the organist could play the "Alleluia Chorus" from Handel's *Messiah* or Wagner's "Ride of the Valkyries."

Oh, there goes Violet like a yard full of peacocks, and now Braden's howling like a villain wrestler with his foot being twisted. Marvelous, yes. When I was in the navy for several days, I made the acquaintance of another recruit who showed me a photo of his baby and said, I made that baby the night I pushed the wall with both feet, man.

Now it seems like they've withdrawn to reorganize their forces, and Mother Pearce's coming back downstairs. Whose deal is it? Oh, mine, and I've already dealt while you all were paying no attention to my wandering reflections.

Mother Pearce came back into the room, saying, Well, well, well, in a loud cheerful tone at total variance with the sharpshooter blaze in her eyes.

What was going on, Mother? asked Gewinner.

Why, nothing at all to speak of, they were just romping and cutting up like a couple of kids when school lets out.

Oh, now, isn't that sweet, said the widow from next door, in a toneless voice.

Partner, have we finished a rubber? Yes? inquired Mother Pearce. Well, why don't we settle the score and have a round of nightcaps for the road.

Mother, suggested Gewinner, why don't we all trot over to the drive-in for a basket of chicken and French fries, since it's so close, so handy?

Now, Gewinner, said Mother Pearce, you'll have to get used to the drive-in when you're home from your travels. It's going to be on that corner for ninety-nine years, at least.

You mean barring a premature blast at The Project, Gewinner murmured. Then he added, louder: Mama, we beat you again, so before you make those nightcaps, shell out eighty-six in greenbacks, and forty-seven in quarters, dimes, nickels and pennies, since my partner and I will not accept your check or an I O U.

He had already risen from the card table and tossed about his shoulders a white silk scarf that was almost the size of a bed sheet and as flawlessly smooth as his skin, and now he was putting on a black topcoat which his bridge partner, the next-door widow, touched with incredulous fingers, and said, Why, that coat is—

She was going to say "moiré" when there came a call at the door, a voice calling out, Delivery from the Drive-in!

Gewinner said, Speak of the devil.

This delivery from the drive-in was, as always, two orders of chicken-in-the-basket with French fries.

That's what Braden always called for when he and Violet had chalked up one more vigorous assault on the huge and dark siege of inertia that can be said to hang about the dynamics of existence—to put it in a somewhat or more than somewhat rhetorical fashion. Just what Braden felt when he had completed one of these furious assaults on the siege of inertia is a question that would have to be put to Braden, and it is doubtful that he would come up with a coherent answer if he tried to give one. The likeliest guess is that he felt like a rooster on a back fence at the sign of daybreak. Anyway one thing is certain. While Braden was still panting from his orgasm, he would pick up the bedroom phone and call the drive-in. Hey, Billy, the same, he would say. Violet would always say, No French fries for me, but Braden would ignore this interjection since a double portion of French fries had never fazed him. At his end of the line, Billy would say, Right over, man, right over!

This delivery from the drive-in was always delivered personally by the proprietor himself. The Laughing Boy, Billy, would carry the two piping-hot baskets straight up to the Braden Pearces' bedroom and he would often stay up there about an hour, having nightcaps with Violet and Braden and reminiscing with Braden about the spectacular tricks and pranks of their boyhood days and nights, such as the Halloween they went in the colored graveyard and dug up a preacher buried the day before and put him and his coffin side by side on the steps of his church along

26

with a big printed sign nailed onto the coffin which said THEY WOULDN'T LET ME IN HEAVEN SO I COME BACK TO PREACH SOME MORE ABOUT HELL TO YOU SINFUL NIGGERS NEXT SUNDAY!

Oh, those were real fun days and nights in their boyhood, and Braden and Billy would assure each other that they were not over yet, no sir, not by a long shot, you could bet on that.

One time Braden said to Billy, I'll tell you something, Buddy, but you forget I told you. Buddy, there's a big Halloween yet to be, but the pranks and the jokes are such classified information, as they call it, that I wouldn't dare even talk about 'em to you, and that's no shit. But this I can say. We've got color TV and on this color TV, Buddy, the blacks and the yellows are coming in so loud and clear that they're burning our eyeballs over at The Project. That much I can till you because you're not a heavy drinker that repeats whatever he hears like a goddamn parrot. I can tell you this big Halloween's coming up, it's necessary like breathing, and after this Halloween, what we're dreaming of at The Project, man, is a white Christmas, and that white-hot snow is gonna fall out of heaven and be as hot as all hell. That much I can tell you and I tell you no lie, and I want you to remember I told you something I wouldn't tell my wife unless she was lying there sleeping dead to the world. Do you dig me?

On that particular night, when the privileged boyhood chum of Braden's went back to close up the drive-in, he had a religious feeling. He felt like he'd been to church and God had delivered the sermon. . . .

This boyhood chum of Braden's, who was still such a chum despite the widely different positions to which fate had assigned them, was named Spangler, Billy Spangler, a lively-sounding name which suited the bearer.

It was just a couple of weeks after Gewinner's return to the bosom of his family, so to speak, that he had his first direct encounter with Billy. It came about in this way. Gewinner did not have wheels of his own at this time but Violet had graciously turned over to him her Caddy convertible which was violet-colored to go with her name, and one fine autumn morning Gewinner impulsively entered the drive of the drive-in for which he had an almost obsessive distaste. He drove into the drive-in without any conscious purpose. He didn't acknowledge to himself that he was intensely curious about Braden's boyhood chum who had that optimistic ninety-nine-year lease on a corner practically facing the Pearce castle.

Gewinner nearly always came on like a cool one despite having a nervous system that kept spitting off hot sparks under his skin as though constantly celebrating a Chinese festival. The late Dr. Horace Greaves had taught Gewinner the secret of outward serenity but his pupil had surpassed the good doctor who would have to go into a state of samadhi when passing through customs in foreign air- or sea-ports. The good doctor's samadhi (a trancelike condition known to Hindu mystics and their disciples) was probably only synthetic since he could enter a customs shed with apparent, dreamlike composure but was apt to go to pieces if a customs officer inquired into the nature of certain pills and vials that were tucked away in his luggage. Then he would come out of samadhi and go directly into something close to hysteria, but Gewinner would lean across the customs counter and say to the officer, My uncle is a saintly man not long for this world, so please don't excite him.

No, Gewinner was not a cool one and yet he could do things that were very disturbing to him and do them with apparent serenity, and so he was able to drive directly up to the entrance of the Laughing Boy Drive-in as smoothly as if he lived there. Violet's Caddy convertible had three silver trumpets for announcing itself in traffic, the trumpets had three different musical notes. Gewinner blew them and Billy Spangler heard them. He recognized the car at once as Violet Pearce's violet-colored Caddy and noticed at once that there was, at the wheel, a young man he had not seen before. He thought he ought to step out of the drive-in to have a closer look at this young man who looked like a boy. He no sooner had this thought than he put it into action and stepped out a pace or two from the door. Then Gewinner had a look at Billy while Billy had a look at him. What Gewinner saw was a young fellow more than ordinarily good-looking with a figure that was lean except for the shoulders which were so heavily muscled that they seemed cramped by the mess jacket of his snowy white uniform. It was a fair-weather day and Billy Spangler seemed to be matching part of the weather. His eyes, looking at Gewinner, had a totally open, aboveboard and straightforward look. He looked like a young man who had never had an *arrière-pensée* in all his life, a young man who started performing an act a second or two before it consciously occurred to him, a young man whose appearance seemed still to reflect, joyfully, the tricks and pranks of his boyhood.

Gewinner was not disarmed by the glowing fair-weather artlessness of Billy's appearance, no, not at all. In fact there was something in the way Billy looked and smiled at him that set off sparklers and spit devils in Gewinner's nervous system, a scorching reminder of various irreconcilables in his nature. And just then the screen door sprang open and out rushed a girl carhop with such momentum that she collided with the back of Billy, let out a screeching laugh and stumbled back against the screen door, exclaiming, Well, I'll be! Excuse me!

Gewinner paid no attention to that little accident, but leaned a bit out of Violet's car and said to Billy, as slowly and precisely as if he were speaking to a retarded child, I would like to have a cup of black coffee, please, just black, no cream and no sugar and no toast or pastry with it.

O.K., said Billy. Then he turned to the girl who

was still against the screen door as if impaled there, and said, Did you get that, honey. She gasped, Yes, and scrambled back into the drive-in.

Billy looked up and about him and shouted, Fine day!

Gewinner made no comment on it.

Then the girl exploded back out of the drive-in with an aluminum tray on which were a cup of piping-hot coffee, a china creamer, two little fluted-paper sugar containers and a glass of ice water. As she brushed past Billy on her way to the car, she let out another little hysterical cry. Billy followed behind her toward the car, walking behind her leisurely and observing her hips in her skintight gabardine slacks, the color of "white coffee." She got to the car and couldn't attach the tray to the door because her fingers shook so, but Billy came up tolerantly beside her and fastened the tray himself. And then he looked down into Gewinner's face and smilingly inquired, Ain't that Mrs. Braden Pearce's new Caddy you're driving there, son?

He did not say it exactly as though he were accusing Gewinner of stealing the car but it was apparent that he was one of the many people who sucked up to Braden. Gewinner's first dislike of the drive-in owner was a reflection of his dislike of his brother, and he ignored the question, coolly disregarded the amiably inquiring eyes and said to the girl, How long has this place been here?

The girl answered nervously, feeling his hostile vibration. She answered in the heavy drawl of the back country. She was freckled, all her features were too small and she had on too much eye pencil and lipstick but her breasts, under the cream-colored silk blouse, and the plushiness of her bottom made it disgustingly plain to Gewinner why this new young buck who owned the drive-in had hired her.

She said, About six months, I think, and her hand shook as she set the ice-water glass down again after removing the napkin underneath it and giving it to Gewinner.

Well, said Gewinner, it's really a shame to put up a thing like this in a residential district!

He said this in a voice that shook like the girl's hand as she set the water glass down. She didn't answer. She made a small noise in her throat and turned quickly away and started back to the little Colonial-style building. But Billy Spangler heard the remark as clearly as Gewinner had intended him to hear it, and he did not follow the girl back into the drive-in but stood leaning easily on the front fender of the new Caddy, glancing lazily back at the girl's hips again as she entered the shiny copper screen door, but then returning his steady gaze to the reddening face of Gewinner. He took his time about responding to Gewinner's attack on his place and the response that he made was quite moderate.

What, he said, is your objection to this drive-in?

It belongs on the highway, said Gewinner.

I thought about the highway, said Billy Spangler,

but this is a lot more convenient for the people that work down there at The Project.

He nodded down the street which the Pearce residence was facing and which led directly up to The Project.

One of Gewinner's great regrets was that intense anger always clouded his mind so that he seldom could think of an immediate and effectually cutting reply to a remark that angered him. Also at such times his voice was always unsteady. Sometimes he even stammered, and so he often had to hold his tongue, and boil inside while he held it. This anger was so intense that at times he felt as though he were on the verge of an epileptic seizure. Now he could not return the look of Billy Spangler nor answer his calm speech nor even lift the coffee cup from the saucer. He was altogether immobilized for possibly half a minute or more while Billy Spangler stared at him and leaned on the Caddy's front fender. All he could do was boil and look down at the coffee while Spangler leisurely went on talking in the same unruffled voice about the advantages of the drive-in's location.

You know, he said, they're doing a mighty big and important job down there at The Project. I don't pretend to know exactly what and I guess it ain't a good thing to be too curious about it unless you're actually in it. But I know from the little I've seen or heard that the whole future security of this country is mixed up with it. Naturally there's got to be some changes in this town that don't suit everybody, like business

33

places cropping up where there used to be private houses and smoke in the air and crowded housing conditions and so many people at the movies you have to stand in line to buy a ticket and then wait again to get to a seat. But all in all, this here's a fast-moving town with business booming. Like Mr. Pearce over there. He's got more different jobs than you can shake a stick at, and not just jobs but the top executive positions. The most important is being in charge of personnel at the plant, but he's sitting on practically every other board or organization in this town. And he's a guy that anybody can talk to. Drops by here every day even if it's just to smile and wave to somebody. And I know *he* don't have no objection at all to this here drive-in, in fact I know that he likes it. I know he likes it because he told me so himself and he leased me the piece of land that the drive-in's built on!

It was then, at this point, that Gewinner flew into action. He came unknotted all at once and he threw the car into gear and started it off before Billy Spangler could even remove his elbow from the fender, so that Spangler was almost knocked off balance and his shoulder was struck by the aluminum tray that was still attached to the rolled-down window of the convertible. He shouted, *Hey!* And Gewinner heard him running along the gravel as if he thought he might overtake the car, but Gewinner did not glance back, he did not even pause to properly remove the tray and its contents, just pushed them off the side of the car as he raced it around the corner on two wheels.

34

There were, of course, repercussions to the incident at the Laughing Boy Drive-in.

That evening Braden came storming up to Gewinner's little apartment in the tower.

Billy Spangler just come over with some fried chicken for me and Violet and he told me his shoulder was sore. I asked him what was wrong with his shoulder and he said he didn't want to tell me but he finally did. He said you went over there today to complain about the drive-in, you hit his shoulder with the tray when you drove out and pitched the tray and the crockery in the street. Now I'd like you to tell me what the shit is the meaning of a thing like this?

Oh, said Gewinner coolly, I believe that the Laughing Boy gave a reasonably accurate report on the incident at the drive-in this morning, but as for the meaning of it, perhaps it just means that Mother and you should not have reduced my travel allowance but kept it at the same level or even increased it.

Gewinner had his back turned to his brother and was ostensibly engaged in cataloguing his big collection of phonograph records, most of which were rare collector's items.

Now look here, Prince!

Yes?

Listen to what I'm telling you for your own good. Nobody comes in this town, not even my brother, without being known and observed and classified by the security counsel at The Project. I mean all unfamiliar persons and types coming here are classified by the new automation system under three headings, "good," "doubtful" or "bad" as security risks. The automation system and the intelligence office check and double-check and triple-check on every newcomer here or anywhere near here. And here's something else for you to know for your own good. New legislation is being pushed through at high speed for the isolation of all you don't-fit-inners, and that word "isolation" can mean several things, none of which things is pleasant for the isolated individual, Prince. There is too much at stake, too much pending, on a worldwide scale for the toleration of temperamental flareups and artistic hoopla, so here's what you do tomorrow. When I go to The Project I'll drop you by the drive-in. You go in there and offer an apology to my friend Billy Spangler, you apologize to him and shake hands with him and pay him for the crockery you broke up, that's what you do in the morning, and face the fact right now that there's got to be some of you don't-fit-inners for a while only, just for a little while till they can be weeded out of society-in-progress, but you are overdoing that privilege which is pro tem only. Understand what I'm saying?

Perfectly, said Gewinner, still coolly, but I would suggest that you save yourself the possible embarrassment of having a brother named Gewinner in isolation, whatever, wherever that is, by arranging with Mother for the restoration of my traveling allowance to its former level or a little higher to meet the inflation problem.

Braden's answer to that was a remark in the nature

36

of obscenity, and the conversation between the brothers was over, it was permanently finished.

Alone in his tower that night, Gewinner opened a window and stood there listening to the faint, perpetual hum of activity at The Project. It moved through the air like the purring of some giant cat that never slept nor changed its menacingly crouched position.

For the first time in his life, as best he could remember, Gewinner thought about good and evil. It seemed to him that he knew, coldly, abstractly, which of the two was which, and also knew which of the two it would suit him better to serve in whatever way it was possible for him to serve it.

He felt a vibration in himself like a countervibration to the one that came from The Project.

I'm being silly, he thought. All I'm here for is to blackmail Mother and Braden into giving me back my travel expenses. What has good and evil got to do with that?

But he stayed at the window and the feeling of two dueling vibrations continued. Hmmm went The Project. Hmmm went Gewinner. And it seemed like an equal conflict, it gave him the sort of strength that a barefooted Hopi, treading bare ground in a dance, is said to draw up out of the blazing dark core of the earth.

Billy Spangler was a very moral guy and he would not have enjoyed his work or gotten nearly so much satisfaction out of the success of the drive-in if he had not been able to think of it as being in its own humble way a part of The Project. It really was in a way. Certainly most if its trade, by far the preponderance of it, came from people directly employed at The Project, and then, of course, virtually everybody and everything else in the town of Gewinner was at least obliquely associated with the Great New Thing. Spangler ran the drive-in as though he was operating a part of The Project, which was not difficult since he was close enough to the outer periphery of The Project's intricate bell system to be apprised of all the changes of shifts the moment that they were effected. When the night shift came on at eight thirty Spangler sent two of his girls home and kept only one on the job, at time and a half, one girl and a colored delivery boy with a bicycle who could carry the occasional calls for hot coffee up to guards who were posted at various points about the key entrances to the grounds. The commissary of the main plant remained open all night so that employees within the buildings did not need to call the drive-in for coffee but the guards could not leave their posts and they preferred their coffee brought in from Billy Spangler's drive-in because the coffee in the commissary was a chronic joke. That's commissary coffee, people would say to Billy when they wanted to tease him, and Billy was very proud of his own coffee. It pleased him to let people know that he lost money on his coffee, he made it so good. A fresh brew of it every hour regardless of how much was still left in the big old electric urns. I throw out more coffee than them drive-ins on the highway make, he would say. I guess it costs me money to serve coffee here, but that's O.K. The best is none too good for the boys down there at The Project.

All this was said so heartily and believed so genuinely that the boastfulness was as lovable as a small boy's. Everybody loved Billy, they thought he was full of fun and a really good Joe. But don't shit around with him, though, especially not any nigger, because ole Billy has got a load of TNT in that left arm of his, and his wiry build is a hell of a lot more powerful than it looks with clothes on.

Billy had done some amateur wrestling on the Monday-night shows that the veterans' organization used to put on at the old Armory building, now torn down and being rebuilt much bigger, and those that had seen Billy wrestle those nights would never forget how he whipped off that purple silk robe with "Billy's Drive-in" inscribed on it and, *Wow,* what a build, holy Jesus, you felt like *shouting* the instant it was uncovered!

This evening Billy Spangler was alone at the drive-in with the new girl whom he had nicknamed Big Edna, not because she was really big but because it happened that one of the other two girls was also named Edna and was so petite that she barely missed being a midget.

This Big Edna, as Billy called her, was the country girl who had served the coffee to Gewinner Pearce

that morning, and she had been shaking with nervousness ever since the awful scene had occurred. Every
once in a while her eyes would turn red, and she
would slip back into the powder room and come out a
minute later looking pale and determined. Billy treat-
ed her gently. He wondered if this was her time of
the month because otherwise he didn't understand
why she took the little occurrence so damn serious. It
didn't really have anything to do with her, it was just
something that happened between him and Mr.
Pearce's eccentric brother which was going to be all
straightened out tomorrow. Mr. Pearce had told him
it would be, and had reaffirmed his approval of the
drive-in and of Billy Spangler and everything else
about it so warmly that the two men had fawned on
each other like a pair of lovers. And Billy Spangler
had repeatedly assured Mr. Braden Pearce that he
wasn't really injured and that it didn't matter a bit
and he wanted him to just forget the whole thing and
he was mad at himself, now, for mentioning a little
occurrence like that to him. It was just that he hated
to think there might ever be any source of misunder-
standing between the drive-in and those wonderful
folks that had leased the property to him. And Billy
knew by the way that Braden Pearce's car swarmed
into the grounds of the Pearce estate that he was
going to raise holy hell with the eccentric brother who
lived in the gray stone tower of the residence. That
was all taken care of.

But the new girl, Big Edna, continued to shake

over it. Now she was still shaking. Perhaps he should
not have kept her on tonight. He worked the girls in
rotation. That is, he worked them overtime in rotation, and this night it was Big Edna's turn to work
overtime but he should have considered her sensitive
feelings and let her go home. He wondered why he
didn't send her home now. It would be surprising if
there were as many as two more customers at the
drive-in between now and closing time at midnight.
Gewinner was a town where serious people (except
for a freak or two like Braden's brother, who sometimes patrolled the streets, empty and dimly lit, in the
convertible Caddy till three or four in the morning as
if he were looking for a pickup) went to bed early
and got up with the chickens. Those were the sort of
hours The Project encouraged its employees and families of employees to keep, and sometimes a man
would be quietly dropped from the rolls for no other
reason than that he was known to be around town on
week nights at late hours. The Project deserved and
got from its men that kind of complete dedication,
Billy Spangler knew that, and nobody respected it
more than he did.

Billy Spangler was conscious of the great social
changes that were now in the air. He felt the glorious
warm wave of the new religiousness and he had made
a bigger contribution than he could afford to the erec-
tion of a new Methodist church which was to have a
swimming pool and badminton courts in the basement and an auditorium that looked like a somewhat

glorified economics classroom. Reform was a mighty good thing and had been a long time coming. It had taken The Project to give everybody in town that serious, dedicated feeling that made them all like so many cells of one great uplifted being. This was a swell way to be and it was no doubt the way toward which the whole progress of mankind had always pointed. It was certainly the ultimate goal of The Project that all the world population of friendly Caucasians were going to have churches like that under the benignly paternal sponsorship of The Center. "The Center" was the new word, rather like a code word, for the immediate locality of The Project. Yes, there were going to be churches like that all over the world, once the great new principle was established and by God and by Jesus everybody was going to have to pitch in and do his bit like Billy Spangler was doing. No more fuck-offs like the sissy Pearce brother. Not here in this country or anywhere in any other country. It's all right to talk about tolerance and individual rights and all of that sort of business but you got to draw a line somewhere. If you give a man too much rope he will hang himself and it was the business of a Christian community dedicated to a Great New Thing to make sure that everybody had just enough rope to keep from being too conscious of confinement and at the same time not enough to tempt the weak ones or the ones that were a little unsettled to self-indulgent excesses of any description.

So Billy Spangler sat on the end of the counter and

watched the new girl, Big Edna, putting the apple-pie slices, left over from the day's business, back into paper cartons so that they could be picked up by the bakery and resold at a discount and Spangler get credit on them. This required a little bending over and each time the girl bent over she flushed a little. She had a brassiere on but not a tight one and her breasts were a good deal bigger than her age and maidenhood seemed to call for. Although Spangler did not talk dirty, sometimes the phrases of his rough boyhood would come into his mind, such as "a pair of ripe boobies." A pair of ripe boobies, he said to himself as he watched her, and the girl cleared her throat and flushed before she spoke to him as if the words in his mind had been spoken aloud.

Now what do I do with these here boxes? she asked him.

He told her just to leave them there on the counter. The bakery boy would pick them up at opening time in the morning.

And then she said, Will that be all, Mr. Spangler?

Yeah, said Billy, you can change out of your uniform now if you want to, honey.

She flushed deeper than ever and nodded her head a little. Then she turned her back to him and self-consciously rooted in her purse for the key to the girl's washroom where the girls left their clothes when they changed. Each of the girls had a key and there were only three of them. Big Edna could not seem to find hers in the purse and he could see her getting sort of

43

panicky about it as she rooted around and still did not locate it. The trouble was that she had too much junk in the pocketbook. She was piling it all on the counter and Billy Spangler had to laugh at her back as he saw all the stuff she had in it, almost the whole cosmetic counter of a five-and-ten, right down to the little two-bit bottle of scent with a colored sweet pea on it. Billy laughed at her back but kept his eyes on her ass most of the time while she was continuing the frantic search for the key. If those gabardine slacks had been a half size smaller, by God, Big Edna could not have gotten into them with a shoehorn, and that was no lie. Billy got up off the counter, slid down off it, rather, and crossed gently over to Big Edna and laid his big hand on her shoulder, for he now perceived that the girl had started crying again, and he said to her gently, Now, honey, you got to stop getting so upset over nothing. That key is in there and if you wasn't so nervous you could find it. Now look here, now. Put all that stuff back in. Yep, that's the ticket, honey. Now give it to me and you go in the gents' room and wash your pretty little face and have a smoke and when you come back I'll have that little door key in the palm of my hand. You want to bet me?

Billy did not mean to let his hand slide down the girl's back, but sometimes a hand does something like that without any plan to. It did. It slid right down her back and onto the curve of her hips and underneath was a softness and a heat that seemed to transfer itself directly from that locality on her body to the frontal

44

equator of his. And now Billy Spangler was the one who felt embarrassed and ill at ease. He flushed and turned his back on Big Edna and returned to the end of the counter with the now tightly packed pocketbook in his hand while she stood there as if she had struck roots in the position she had been in when his rebellious hand had made the inadmissable breach of consideration. For the hand of Billy Spangler had just now violated one of his firmest principles of conduct, which was never to take advantage of any opportunity that seemed to be offered by a female employee.

In Billy's defense it ought to be noted that he was a twenty-seven-year-old bachelor and had not been to bed with a girl since weeks ago when the Public Relations Committee at The Project had given little Eula Mayberry her train fare home. Eula had been the last survivor of the once thriving industry of prostitution which was one of the things that The Project had cleaned up in its drive to make the community worthy in every respect of the Great New Thing of which it was now The Center. Billy was planning to marry as soon as he found the right girl but in the meantime he didn't want to run the risk of getting mixed up with a wrong one because there is nothing that can bitch up a man's whole life worse than an unwise marriage can. There was ample evidence in Billy's life of the appeal that he had for bad women, and Billy believed that there were just two kinds of women, the good and the bad kind, and somehow it seemed like it was the bad kind that took the biggest interest in Billy. It seemed like he couldn't come near one of them kind of women without their reaching a hand out or trying to make him do it.

Well, it just wouldn't do. Billy had ambitions and matrimony was a definite part of his ambitions. He was going to find him a good little girl on a social level that was distinctly higher than his own had been. Maybe he'd have to wait four or five years for that to happen. Maybe it would not happen until after he had opened two or three more drive-ins and was an absolutely unmistakably up-and-coming young potentate of the commercial and social scene. But it was going to happen, it was bound to come. Patience and Spartan fortitude were required in the meantime, and incidentally it was necessary to allow himself to jerk off once a week in order to keep himself from going around all the time with a half-erection in those white pants to make the customers snicker. Tonight was the night for him to practice that melancholy little act of abasement and it made him sort of sweetly sad inside just thinking about it, knowing how much sweeter and better-feeling it was to do the other thing, which there were so many wonderful chances to do. But The Project called for men with characters of rock. And Billy thought of himself as being a part of The Project, still a humble part of it, but one that was on the right track to arrive someday, through humility and obedience and Spartan control of himself, at a position of far greater eminence and much closer to The Center than he now was.

Billy Spangler could not keep his mind on what he was supposed to be doing with the girl's pocketbook, which was looking for the lost key. Piece by piece and very, very slowly he removed the contents from the pocketbook but even if he had come across the key it is doubtful that he would have noticed it. All the while he was listening. He heard the girl undressing in the gents' washroom which was right back of where he was standing, and then he heard her put the toilet seat down and then he heard the flow of her urination and he wondered, if she had the rag on, if she were going to change it in there. But of course she wasn't going to. How could she? In the girls' washroom they had a Kotex dispenser but there was nothing but paper towels and toilet tissue in the men's. He wondered if she would have forgotten about that and have to try to put the old one back on or pad herself down there with toilet paper or coarse paper towels. But of course if she was that absent-minded she would probably have flushed the old one down the toilet when she finished peeing. Now he heard her finish and the toilet flush and if she had actually made that mistake she would now be about to realize it. Billy Spangler listened. He just couldn't help it. He stood there waiting and listening with her dusty, sweet-smelling pocketbook in his hand and even the pocketbook seemed to smell of the young girl's darkly crimson incubative condition.

And then Billy Spangler moved to the gents'-room door. A great flow of air or water seemed to have

swept him toward it—and the door, too—it pushed
the door open, and there she was in the very condition
in which his vivid intuition had shown her, naked
from the waist down, a hand containing a wad of
tissue paper clapped over the blond-haired groin and
her face contorted with the beginning of tears. Billy
heard himself saying out loud to her, but very softly,
There, there, there, don't cry, you mustn't cry, baby!
And the hand that he now put on her was made out
of steel. His knees felt a thud as they hit on the concrete floor but after that he didn't feel anything that
wasn't the plushy feel and heat and smell and taste of
the sobbing girl's body.

The following morning Billy Spangler fired her. It
was very, very clear to him now that Big Edna was
the bad kind of girl. He did not believe that she had
lost the key. He wasn't took in by that story. She was
a country girl but she knew what she was up to when
she pretended to be so scared and nervous, and not if
he lived to be a thousand years old would he ever get
over the dreadful degradation of what she had got
him to do. He was not mean to her. This was not his
way of doing a thing. He gave her a full week's pay,
although she had only worked three days and a night,
and he asked her if that was enough to get her back
home to the hill town that she had come from the
week before. He said goodbye to her nicely, even
shook hands with her and said, Honey, what you
should do is go and have a talk with the minister of
your church. Tell him your problem. Always go to a

man with the light of God in him when you get tempted by your animal nature. He said that to her in all sincerity and kindness because it was now completely apparent to Billy Spangler that it had been the animal nature of the girl, her devil, that had perpetrated the terrible misdeed, not his, not any part of his nature, for Billy knew that he had been brought to Jesus six years ago by an army chaplain in the jungles of Wangtsee.

When Billy turned around from the telephone over which he had just inserted an advertisement for a new girl in the *Courier-Times,* he saw that the tall young man who had entered behind his back and taken a seat at the counter was the Pearce boy, Gewinner, the one that had been responsible for yesterday's trouble.

The two men looked at each other. Billy felt his own face turning as cold and set as the face of the man sitting down, and he did not try to prevent himself from assuming a hard expression because he felt it was called for. Nevertheless he had to remember that this fellow was at least nominally a member of the Pearce family that had leased him the land on which the drive-in was built. Outside Billy saw the car of Braden Pearce waiting and the fine younger brother himself at the wheel of it, with an escort of two motorcycle cops standing by. Billy knew what had happened. Braden Pearce had compelled his brother to come here and make an apology to him for what had happened. Braden had literally dragged him over to make the apology and the restitution now coming up. So then Billy Spangler relaxed himself a little. He let the hard expression slip down from his face and he took a seat beside Gewinner and told the girl at the counter to give him some coffee.

Then he turned around and said to the other man, Well, son, I hope you like our coffee better today than you did yesterday morning. Leisurely he removed his jacket, rolled up his white poplin sleeve and showed the purplish bruise on his biceps where the tray had struck him as the car drove off. He just showed it and looked down at the other man's face which still had not spoken or altered its set expression.

Well, said Billy, there is no hard feelings between me and any member of the family you belong to and never will be as long as your brother, Braden, and I have got anything to do or say about it. I reckon you come in here to make an apology to me. But I want you to know you don't have to make it. All you have to do is set there and drink your coffee and leave the girl a dime tip!

With this benevolent speech still on his lips, Billy Spangler elevated his hips from the white porcelain stool and started out toward the sunshiny exterior to shake hands with Braden Pearce. But before he had completed the beginning of his easy movement, he heard a spitting sound. He did not quite turn around but he knew what had happened. Gewinner Pearce had spit in his cup of coffee. Billy had seen the quick snakelike jerking forward of the head of Gewinner and the startled look on the face of Little Edna and heard the sound of the spitting all at once. Billy was motionless. He stayed in a frozen position, half looking out toward the car of Braden Pearce and half regarding the crouched figure of Braden's brother. While he stayed immobilized that way, Gewinner had taken out his wallet. He set on the counter a hundred-dollar bill and then he said quietly, I am not the type that leaves a dime tip!

Almost immediately after he made that speech, in fact with the words still on his lips, he swept past Billy Spangler. The smooth, plushy sleeve of his light-tan overcoat brushed against Billy's bare arm as Gewinner swept past him, and Billy saw him go on out of the drive-in and cut rapidly across the street, not even turning to look at his brother's car.

Apparently only two people, besides Gewinner, knew that Gewinner Pearce had not apologized but had spit in his cup of coffee. Little Edna knew it and Billy Spangler knew it. They glanced at each other. Little Edna had a tight, scared face as she seized a wet dishcloth and wiped the counter, and Billy Spangler, for the first time in his adult life, had a feeling of fear, of anxiety cold and deep, way down in his warm young bowels, making them cold, and with it was also a touch of awe and revulsion.

Hey, Prince, called Braden to Gewinner, but Gewinner ignored him and stalked out to the street. Then Braden called out, Hey, Billy.

Billy came out of the drive-in like a man stumbling

out of a bomb-shattered building, in a state of shock or concussion; he came out with his jaws a little ajar and a sightless look in his baby-blue eyes.

Well, what happened, did the prick apologize to you? I want to know the truth, now.

Somehow Billy couldn't report the truth of the weird thing that had happened inside, all he could do was jerk his head affirmatively and raise a hand as if saluting or bestowing a blessing.

O.K., that's that, shouted Braden and his bullet-proof limousine shot forward, preceded by two motorcycle cops with screaming sirens, reaching The Project before Gewinner reached the imitation drawbridge of the Pearce castle.

Gewinner assumed that there was bound to be another confrontation scene with his brother that evening and he thought he would show his boldness by coming downstairs for it. However, it so happened that Braden and Mother Pearce had hopped off by helicopter to the State Capitol in order to appear at the deathbed of the Governor who had been shot down unexpectedly while laying the cornerstone of the Trust in God Mission Building.

Gewinner got this information from the butler in the great downstairs hall.

Then nobody's in, he reflected aloud.

Yes, me, in the gameroom, called out Violet.

He found her in there with a tall crystal shaker and

a long silver spoon, stirring a considerable number of cocktails, apparently for one person which was herself.

I didn't go along with Braden and Mother Pierce, she told him somewhat unnecessarily.

Oh? Why not?

Because the whirlybird makes me so dizzy that I can't walk a straight line when I get off it. I guess it's just not my type of locomotion. Will you have a martin?

Is that some variation on a martini?

It's a boatload of martinis laced with a dash of absinthe, which is illegal in this country, but dear old Senator Connor got it through customs by putting a rum label on the bottle when he came back from his talks with General Amados in Rio, just a few days before he had his last stroke in Vegas.

She said all this so quickly and brightly that you might have thought she was making plans for Christmas, and Gewinner found himself feeling more at home with her than ever.

Do you mind if I take off my dinner jacket? he asked her.

I don't care if you take off everything you've got on.

I won't go as far as that, said Gewinner, removing only his jacket.

While she was chilling the martinis, he commented on the unseasonable warmth of the castle. He said:

53

You know the castle is always overheated because Mother Pearce has anemia and control of the thermostat.

Oh, do I know! said Violet. Isn't she the cutest little thing? She goes around in her little Angora wool sweater as if she was always chilly in the castle and she keeps on turning the thermostat up a notch higher.

Maybe she wants to sweat us out.

That's a thought, agreed Violet.

Her next remark was something in the nature of a *non sequitur*.

This room, she said, isn't bugged. The library is bugged and so are the dining room and the conservatory. This room used to be bugged but something went wrong with the bugging apparatus just a few minutes after Braden and Mother Pearce went out of the castle *ce soir*.

Are you sure about that?

I'm as sure about that as if I'd broke it myself, so you and I can talk on any subject we choose.

Is there something in particular you wanted to discuss with me? asked Gewinner.

Excuse me for a moment, she said.

She went to a window and opened it to admit a pigeon that had a piece of paper attached with a rubber band to one leg. She removed the paper and scanned it hastily while the pigeon waited, either nervously or restlessly, on the billiard table.

Intuitively Gewinner decided that this was an occurrence which it was best to pretend not to notice.

Hmmm, said Violet.

Then she rolled the piece of paper into a ball which she dropped in her cocktail and swallowed. She then tore off a sheet of paper from a memo pad on the bar and scribbled rapidly on it. That done, she whistled to the pigeon which flapped over to the bar and held a leg out for the return message and the rubber band.

All this went off quite smoothly and in less than a minute the pigeon was flapping back out the window.

Violet looked more amused than bemused.

I don't know how Mother Pearce can possibly imagine that I could be so stupid as not to realize that she is promoting a match between your brother and Babe. I'd be so willing to surrender Braden to Babe that if I was a licensed justice of the peace or an ordained minister of the church I would be delighted to bind them together in holy matrimony. However, it's necessary for me to remain in the castle a little bit longer because of my appointment.

Violet, said Gewinner, you are a very unusual girl.

Thank you, she said, so are you. Oh, excuse me, I don't mean a girl, I mean unusual, honey.

Where are you from?

Oh, from a long time ago, was her somewhat mysterious answer.

Then she went on talking.

The calisthenics at night, she said, are making the skin of my body look like a boatload of orchids and I have a funny feeling that when Braden succumbs to the attractions of Babe, he's going to look like a boat-load of orchids himself, because I think Babe, with her stomp and all, is a personality like a whole foot-ball team condensed into one single being. Why do I feel I can talk to you so freely?

Because the room isn't bugged?

Oh, that isn't it. I think what it is, is you are some kind of a changeling, something else, not of this world, you know.

Thank you, said Gewinner. May I ask you about the pigeon bit?

Of course you can. I have an old school chum named Gladys who thinks that the most obvious and discreet method of exchanging messages is by carrier pigeons. Would you like her to send you a little message that way?

What kind of message?

Oh, she'd think of something.

At this moment there was a terrific clatter in the hall that built to a climax when an unusually fat little girl bounced or bounded, or both, into the gameroom, and immediately began to heckle Violet.

Mommy Violet drinks too much, Mommy Violet drinks too much!

That's Mommy Violet's business, not yours, pre-cious.

The child stuck out her tongue at her mother and at Gewinner in very rapid succession, and then rushed over to the slot machine that paid off in gumdrops. She hit the jackpot at the first try and howled with insane delight.

What is the name of this strange child? asked Gewinner.

Why, I don't remember, all I remember about her is that after the first look at her I got myself what they call a diaphragm and regard it as my dearest earthly possession.

Child, said Gewinner, if you like candy, run up to the tower and look around for a great big box up there. It's full of marshmallows and chocolate cherries and marzipan and divinity flavored with strychnine.

Oh goody good, screamed the child and clattered off to the tower without even asking what the strange words meant, having understood "candy."

Violet talked to Gewinner about The Project.

It seemed that Braden had gotten carried away by a mood of boastfulness one night and had bragged to Violet that it would soon be possible to possess and control the whole planet by pressing a button connected with a wire. You just pressed the button connected with the wire and the whole fucking thing would either be blown to bits or fall under the absolute dominion of The Project, and he, said Braden, was the one who would press the button when the delicacies and intricacies of the contraption were completely mastered.

Yes, but suppose, said Gewinner, reflectively, Braden did push the button but somebody else had cut the little wire?

I love you, said Violet, and I see that you love Braden as much as I do.

Yes, I would love to be there when he pressed the

57

little button and it dawned on his sensitive mind that someone had cut the little wire. . . .

There was not such a thing as a periodic spy scare in the town of Gewinner, now grown to a city. The scare was not periodic, it was constant. The Project and the town-city were haunted by it the way old people are haunted by dread of disease. Nobody came into The Project without going through an exhaustive screening process. It is not likely that anybody came into the town without being investigated or secretly watched. Everybody knew that there were a lot of plain-clothes detectives around the town. They called them the PeeCees, and whenever you saw somebody you didn't know standing around on a corner with an air of elaborate unconcern you could be pretty damn sure it was one of those PeeCees, and if he gave you a glance it was likely to loosen your bowels.

Anxiety was the occupational disease of The Project employees. There was a neurological hospital on the grounds and a whole staff of psychiatrists. Of course, as soon as a man showed signs of severe nervous unbalance he had to be let out, but God knows how many of the men were concealing little foxes of terror under their radiationproof uniforms and helmets, anxieties growing into psychoses which they dared not speak of. The staff of doctors walked around with their hands clasped behind them, waiting for patients who were afraid to come in. Not till somebody actually broke down with the screaming meemies was the

58

cat out of the bag, and then of course it was too late. He was hustled out of The Project and out of the town and sent to what they called Camp Tranquillity, which was supposedly a place of readjustment. The place did not have a very savory reputation among The Project employees. There were ugly rumors about it, rumors of people who went there and never were heard of again, at least not after the first hysterically gay postcard saying, *This place is heaven!* The rumors were never completely authenticated. But you must remember that even the mail coming into the town of Gewinner was screened by a special staff of postal employees. It was not opened. It was examined by a sort of fluoroscope machine, every letter or package that came into the town was examined this way. All that anyone knew for certain was that the first postcard (from the worker sent to Camp Tranquillity) was also the last. If inquiries were addressed to the camp by former friends of the worker, a form letter would be delivered in precisely five days, saying that So-and-so had made a remarkably rapid recovery and had graduated to Rancho Allegro, which was located somewhere in the Southwest—for some reason nobody ever found out exactly where.

It must be remembered about all this that the workers at The Project were extremely busy people, they had practically no time for contemplation and had been chosen for their jobs because they were not introverts, and if they developed introspective tendencies it was certainly not to their advantage to make a public show of them or even a private one. They were better off than any other skilled workers or unskilled workers in the country, especially since the dissolution of the major unions by a recent Act of Congress. They occupied model houses for which they paid a nominal rent and they were retired at the age of forty-five on a comfortable pension to certain segregated communities called Rainbow Lands and Bluebird Hills and Valleys where everybody was about the same age and everyone from the barber to the mortician was a state employee and all the bills were sent to Mr. Whiskers.

Nothing to worry about in Gewinner! That was the cry. No reason for any grouches. No reason for anybody to wear anything but a radiationproof outfit and a happy smile. In fact, there was a ban on blues music in the town, and the government had established a Happy Song Center where a staff of composers devoted themselves to the composition of light-hearted ballads. There was never a lyric that didn't mention silver linings, blue birds, sunshine and smiles. These records were on all the café Wurlitzers and the disk jockeys played nothing else. But as I said already, one thing that wasn't mentioned, but that everybody thought about in secret, was the ever-menacing idea of *"the spy."* It interfered with really close and warm relationships among members of The Project community. You never knew, did you? No matter how simple and good a guy might seem to be, who knows but what he was a counterspy, taking notes on you all the time and the notes going into the files of the office that had the big wide-open blue eye painted on the opaque glass of its entrance, and nothing more.

Nobody could be more conscious of the spy threat than was Billy Spangler, and whenever he was screening a possible new employee at the drive-in, he turned on his intuitive powers with terrific concentration. Billy thought that he had singular powers along that line, he thought he was someone who had a real, native instinct about the characters of people, oh, not based on anything scientific but just, well, just a matter of natural sensibility, of aptitude for that sort of thing.

Now this particular morning, which was the morning after Gewinner Pearce had spit in his coffee at the drive-in, and a classified ad for a new waitress had gone into the papers, Billy Spangler was interviewing a number of teen-age girls for the vacancy. Billy knew, that for business reasons, the girl had to be a good-looker as well as efficient and sprightly. "Personable" was the word he used in the ad: Vacancy for lively, personable girl-waiter. Experience less important than background and character.

You may wonder why he used "girl-waiter" instead of "waitress" in the ad. Billy's use of that less usual term was because the word "girl" was a word that was almost continually in the simple heart of Billy. Girl, girl, girl. The word haunted him even more persistently than the idea of spies and counterspies in the town and The Project.

Sometimes when he was not thinking at all—and such times were not infrequent, Billy Spangler not being primarily a man of intellectual nature—at those times the word would hop into his thought without any apparent chain of associations, just the word, Girl, girl! And he would whisper it to himself and saliva would fill his mouth as he whispered it. Then he would catch himself. He would look around quickly and swallow. And he would glance self-consciously down the front of his trousers and edge behind the counter of the drive-in or the cashier's box until his emotion had subsided a little. So the request for a girl-waiter had gone into the papers and there were at least a dozen applicants for the job, mostly girls of high school age or a little older who were daughters of men in The Project.

There were two key questions in Billy Spangler's method of screening a possible new employee at the drive-in. Number one: What is your opinion of Gloria Butterfield? That was the name of a famous spy at The Project who had been caught by The Eye as she was on her way to deliver a set of blueprints into the hands of enemy agents in a nearby town, two old women and a man, who were posing as relatives of hers, one of whom pretended to be ill. The whole bunch was apprehended, of course. It was a very hush-hush affair, no public trial, only the barest comment in the newspapers, but of course word about it was whispered in conversation and it had never been officially denied that Gloria Butterfield and her associates had come to a particularly unhappy end which was something a little more colorful than capital punishment.

They didn't shoot no gun, they didn't cut no string. But one thing you can be sure of. Nobody's ever going to see the face of Gloria Butterfield again on *this* earth.

That was the slow and sententious way that Billy Spangler spoke of it. He gave the impression of knowing more about it than anybody else. When Gloria Butterfield was discussed, there was always some allusion to what Billy Spangler said. He was the unofficial expert on the case. He knows a whole lot about it that he's not saying, was the popular opinion. And this Gloria Butterfield case, and his pretentiously cryptic utterances about it, had vastly enhanced the prestige of Billy Spangler as a sort of oracle upon the subject of spies.

So much for screening question number one. If the girl passed it, that is, if she expressed a suitably adverse opinion on Gloria Butterfield and a sufficiently enthusiastic endorsement of the unknown but radical manner in which Gloria had been (allegedly) disposed of, Billy Spangler would then come up with his number-two inquiry which was very simple indeed: How do you feel about love? Usually the girls would relax a little and so would Billy when he asked this question. He would smile and expose his white teeth, teeth so perfect that they looked like a set of beautiful dentures except that you saw quite clearly that they

63

were fitted into his healthy pink gums by nature. He would not only expose his beautiful teeth and gums when he asked this question but he would open his mouth sufficiently to expose the whole interior of his coral-pink mouth, glittering with spit like the interior of some little coral cave on the seashore that was filled and emptied to the rhythm of the tides. You saw his rather small pink tongue, the pink of which was a little darker than the pink of the gums, the tip of which was actually crimson and so smooth that the taste buds on it were almost invisible. It was like an artificial tongue of pink and crimson it was so perfect. And so when Billy Spangler opened his mouth and smiled and let his mouth hang a bit open after that foxy question, the girls would laugh with a little burst of pure joy, feeling that the really serious part of the interview was over. But actually Billy Spangler was still screening the girls at this point. Although the question appeared to be a light one and was asked in a playful manner, a wrong answer to it could terminate the whole interview on a very quick and negative note indeed. It was a serious question with Billy Spangler what the girls thought about love. He did not want a girl who thought too much about it nor did he want a girl who showed a neurotic antipathy to the idea of it. He wanted a girl to show a wholesomely light and joyous attitude toward it, as an abstract value, the sort of attitude that a boy has learned to expect from his mother, for instance. A clean-minded, openhearted attitude toward love in the abstract was what he looked for. And if, when he asked that question, the girl dummied up, he would know that something was amiss and he would say, Sorry, next girl!

Now on this particular morning Billy Spangler was upset about things. He had not felt really well since the incident with Gewinner Pearce, and the thing that had happened that night with Big Edna had been a severe psychic jolt although it had ended in a moral victory on his part. That is, he had shown the firmness of character to give her the sack the next day. But this morning the interviews had not gone well. The girls were an indifferent-looking bunch for one thing, only one of them being what you would call a real looker. There was a sameness about them, a blank kind of neatness and trimness which made you feel a bit let down somehow. Sexiness was what they lacked, although Billy Spangler would hesitate to put it quite that way.

This applied to all of the girls but one. One of them it did not apply to, not even slightly. That girl was a regular looker, a really outstanding good-looker, she was personable *plus,* and Billy had interviewed her first of the lot. But there was something not quite right in her reaction to the number-one question about Gloria Butterfield. She had betrayed no nervousness. Without a ghost of a hesitation she had said right off that she thought that Gloria Butterfield was a thoroughly contemptible person, not only ignoble but stupid, stupid because she had allowed herself to be caught at her ignoble action. And she certainly deserved what she got. Any girl who would be that treacherous and that stupid deserved to be torn to pieces by wild dogs.

Now what bothered Billy Spangler was how this girl happened to make the remark about Gloria Butterfield being torn to pieces by wild dogs. Billy had never spoken of this bit of information. He knew of it from Braden Pearce, but under oath of secrecy, and only because of the extremely close buddy-relationship that he enjoyed with the great man across the road. He had never breathed a word of it to anybody and he was pretty goddamn certain that Braden would never have passed the information along to anyone else not in the inner circle of The Project. The fact that the girl betrayed her knowledge of it gave him quite a turn. He was noticeably startled when she came out with that remark. He thought he covered up his surprise pretty well but he could feel his face burning as he went quickly on to the next question, What do you think about love? The pretty girl's answer to that one was also just a little bit offbeat.

She looked Billy Spangler right straight in the eyes without the flicker of an eyelash and she said to him, Well, frankly, I have not had much experience with it but I think the idea is great!

No, that wasn't quite the way for a girl to answer the second question, but it was not seriously wrong. It was the answer to the Gloria Butterfield question that disturbed him, and yet Billy Spangler somehow could

66

not bring himself to dismiss the girl immediately. He knew that he *should* but he *didn't*.

What he said to the girl—to quote him exactly— was, Stick around a little.

Where? she asked him, and he told her to sit down at the end of the counter and have a cup of coffee and a sandwich.

The girl smiled brightly and obeyed his instructions and Billy's eyes followed her body as it moved away from him. She had on a checkered wool skirt that fitted her real close across the hips and the hips were the shape that he had liked in Big Edna so fatally well, except that they were just a little bit smaller and possibly firmer. The breasts were even superior to Big Edna's. "Ripe boobies" was not exactly the word for her breasts in that shameful secret vocabulary of Billy's. No, a perfect phrase for them was "A nice handful!"

Well, the interviews went along pretty briskly but Billy found something wrong with each one of the other applicants, and inside of half an hour the girl who gave the wrong Gloria Butterfield answer was the only one left of the bunch. She had finished her coffee and she had also ordered a piece of butterscotch graham pie, which is a pie that is very rich and gooey with a crust of graham crackers, certainly not a dessert that a girl would order if she had any apprehensions about her figure. This girl obviously had none. What a trim little figure she had on her, and the breasts were a nice little handful and that was for sure. She had now pivoted around on the counter stool and was smiling expectantly the length of the drive-in at Billy Spangler who had planted himself self-consciously behind the cash register now that he found himself alone with her. It was the slow part of the morning now, the part between ten and twelve, and the two girls already working were sitting outside on the bench in front of the drive-in, looking fresh and inviting as Billy always expected his girls to do. So now there was plenty of time to give this applicant a really close screening. She had so much to recommend her, and the odd surprise that she had handed him on the Gloria Butterfield question might be very simply and easily explained.

Now, honey, he said—always treating his girls with that sort of comfortable affectionate familiarity like a big brother's—you said one thing that bothered me a little and I guess you know what it was. Now how did you happen to mention the "wild dogs" thing?

The girl stopped smiling. Oh, she said. She got up from the counter and started toward the door, her face looking flushed and her movements rather jerky.

Where are you going, asked Billy.

Home, said the girl. I don't think I want a job bad enough to work for a man who might be suspicious of me!

Now hold your horses, said Billy. You are going off half-cocked. Just because I was a little surprised because you knew of something that is known of by only a few people very closely connected with The Project is no good reason for you to blow up and say I am being unduly suspicious of you.

He had crossed to the door. The girl was trying to open it but Billy Spangler was leaning against it so that she couldn't.

Again the girl looked him straight in the eyes. Do you or do you not think I can be trusted? she demanded in a sharp tone.

Trusted? Why, honey, I'd bank every cent in my possession on that smile of yours, said Billy, that wonderful frank and open smile of yours and that pair of baby-blue eyes! Now you let go of that door and sit back down and—*Henry!*—he called in to the Negro cook in the kitchen.

Henry, he called, how about that fresh coffee? Bring two cups out here, and bring me out a piece of that fresh apple pie!

Billy Spangler was all smiles, he was wreathed in cherubic smiles that made him look like a butch and tender angel of honest-to-goodness young, sweet, pure-hearted manhood.

The girl responded. Who wouldn't? She sat back down again and opened her mouth so that Billy could look right into the coral pink interior of it, as wet and smooth as his own. Consciously at that moment he caught himself thinking about a French kiss, and as the coffee and apple pie were set in front of him, Billy Spangler had to cross his legs. But the girl did not stop smiling and she did not shut her mouth till

Billy asked her what size shoes and uniform she took. Then she shut her mouth for a moment in order to speak.

Oh, she said, then I have got the job?

Yes indeed, she had it. . . .

All at once, in early February, there was an outbreak of crime in the town of Gewinner, interrupting a long period of such extreme orderliness that during the preceding year no misdemeanor has been committed of a nature more serious than the theft of an artichoke from a chain grocery. The first evidence of the crime wave was the discovery of a billfold that had been ripped apart and dropped at the entrance of an alley. This was like the first eruption of some epidemic pox, for within a few nights the ripped-up billfolds had increased to a score. Then to a hundred. The crimes were flawlessly executed. At least half of the victims were solitary patrolmen, assaulted upon their midnight rounds of the deserted downtown streets, and none of them could give a really satisfactory account of what had happened. They had seen or heard nothing to arouse suspicion or even particular attention prior to the knockout blow, delivered invariably to the back of the head, in some cases with such violence that the skull was fractured. It was like a big black cat had jumped on me, one of them asserted, and from this statement was derived the name "Black Cat Gang" that was fastened on the criminals. The victims who were not patrolmen were

70

workers returning home from the nocturnal shifts at
The Project. At first, workers in vehicles enjoyed
immunity from the attacks and consequently an order
was issued that no pedestrians would be permitted on
the streets of Gewinner after 8 P.M. But almost immediately after this edict, a number of workers were
found unconscious at the wheels of their cars, everything of value stripped from them, along the curbs of
the residential sections. It was then ordered that no
private vehicle should be operated at night containing
less than two passengers; the police force was multi-
plied by ten and the streets were illuminated by giant
lamps that gave a ghastly greenish hue to everything
that they shone upon. Crime experts flooded into the
city. Great banners were hung in the streets listing the
precautions that were to be taken by the night workers
of The Project: Drive well to the center of the street
. . . slow down but do not stop at street intersections
. . . maintain a uniform speed of twenty-five miles
an hour in the business section and forty miles an
hour in the residential sections . . . keep to the main
thoroughfares wherever it is possible . . . do not pick
up strangers under any circumstances, etc. Then during the last week of February a council meeting was
held at which the investigating committee disclosed
that the leader of the Black Cat Gang was none other
than the Chief of Police. This encouraging bit of information was not released to the press but rumors of
it leaked out and the effect on the civil population was
rather demoralizing. Nocturnal life in the town got to

be like one big continual wild West movie until the whole police force was sent to Camp Tranquillity and was replaced by government agents in armored cars. Then, at least on the surface, the town and The Project fell back into the former well-ordered pattern of existence. A record number of religious converts were made by all the churches and optimists in the pulpits referred to the crime wave, now under control, as "the Devil's Last Stand."

Gewinner Pearce loved most the hours between midnight and dawn, when only the graveyard shift at The Project was still awake. From his tower windows, with lights extinguished, he would watch until he saw the drive-in closed and Billy Spangler driving home in his neat little green coupe. Then Gewinner would prepare to go out. He did not dress warmly. He liked a feeling of chill which made him more conscious of the self-contained life in his body. Chill air about his limbs made them move more lightly, more buoyantly, and so he went out thinly clad. He wore no undergarments. All that he wore on his nocturnal prowlings was a midnight-blue tuxedo made of silk gabardine. Before getting into this garment Gewinner would bathe and anoint himself like a bride, standing among a maze of indirectly lighted mirrors in his shower room. His whole body would be sprayed with pine-scented eau de Cologne and lightly dusted with powder. Gossamer silk were his socks, nylons of the sheerest ply, and his shoes weighed hardly more than a pair of gloves. Crystalline drops cleared his eyes of fatigue, brushes polished the impeccable enamel of his teeth and an astringent solution assured his mouth and throat of an odorless freshness. Often this ritual of preparation would include internal bathing with a syringe, a warm enema followed by a cold one, for Gewinner detested the idea of harboring fecal matter in his lower intestines. He wore a single metal ornament which was a Persian coin, very ancient, that hung on a fine silver chain. He enjoyed the cold feeling of it as it swung pendulumlike across his ribs and bare nipples. It was like carrying a secret, and that was something that Gewinner liked better than almost anything in the world, to have and to keep a secret. He also had the romantic idea that someday, some galactic night, he would find the right person to whom to make a gift of the coin. That person had not been found, never quite, and there was the sad but endurable possibility that the discovery would be postponed forever, but in the meantime the Persian coin was a delicately exciting reminder of the fact that night is a quest.

Once or twice when he had only recently resumed his residence in the town, Gewinner was accosted by patrolmen and asked for identification. Now the patrolmen knew him, they knew Gewinner and they knew Violet's Caddy. They might theorize about the mystery of his prowlings but no interference was offered, such was the power of the name that he bore and the curiously intimidating aura of his person.

Gewinner's night prowling followed a certain pattern. At a leisurely pace, always five miles less than the official speed limit for the confines of the municipality, he would pass down the main thoroughfare of the town, appearing, whenever he paused at a crossing, to look around for somebody. All the windows and doorways were locked and lightless. Every three or four blocks he would pass a patrolman who gave him a single, quick glance, full of alarm and discretion, which Gewinner boldly returned with a very slight nod, as though he were an inspector signifying a routine approval of their presence upon the sidewalks. When he arrived at the end of the main avenue, he would turn Violet's Caddy (now always at his disposal) to the right and proceed along a street of new and completely uniform cottages which had been put up by The Project. This street terminated at the athletic stadium of the high school, and there Gewinner would always stop for a while. Sometimes he would remain in the parked car, close to the main gate of the open stadium, and take a few puffs of a cigarette which he would extinguish as soon as the car started off once more. But sometimes he would get out of the car and stroll to the water fountain inside the stadium. He would appear to drink though he never allowed the water to touch his lips. Then he would stand beside the fountain a minute or two, looking about the dark stands which were seldom quite empty. His eyes would sweep along the whole oblong of the open-air structure until the glow of a

74

cigarette at some point would betray another visitor's presence. Gewinner would then remove from the pocket of the topcoat, never worn but carried across his arm, a white silk scarf which he would unfold and spread over a concrete bench that was close to the water fountain. Then he would sit down and wait. This was not in keeping with the convention of the place—for all such places have their peculiar conventions—and more often than not Gewinner would wait in vain. If he grew impatient but was still hopeful, he would take out a silver lighter and a cigarette. He would hold the flame of the lighter before his face for a count of ten, not lighting the cigarette, just holding the flame a little away from the tip. Then he would wait a while longer, and sometimes, reluctantly, fearfully, the one who had made the firefly glow in the distance would emerge from the stands and approach the fountain. When this stranger had arrived within a few feet of the fountain and Gewinner had obtained some impression of his general aspect, Gewinner would either rise abruptly and make a rapid exit from the stadium or else he would cross to the fountain just as the stranger arrived there and murmur a word or two as the stranger bent to drink. When this was the procedure, the following step was invariable. Side by side and moving rapidly, Gewinner and the stranger, now his companion, would cross wordlessly out of the stadium and to the parked car. The car would then abandon its former pretense of languor and would shoot rapidly through the sleeping

community, out to a certain road that Gewinner had
known in his boyhood, a road that terminated for his
purposes in the Negro cemetery about two miles out
of town, and there among the humble mossy tablets
and weather-paled crosses of wood, in a certain covert
among them, surrounded by winter rosebushes,
Gewinner would unfold the silk scarf again to its full
length and width which gave it the dimensions of a
bed sheet. Silently, never speaking, he would unclothe
himself, standing immediately before the trembling
stranger and staring directly and fiercely into the
stranger's eyes, breathing upon his face his fragrant
breath and dropping his clothes at his feet till he was
quite naked; then, finally, not quite smiling, but low-
ering his eyes and turning half in profile as though he,
too, were suddenly abashed by the strange occurrence,
then he would murmur, *Well? Am I too ugly?*

Certainly Billy Spangler did not reconsider the hiring of the new girl, Gladys, but the night after he
hired her was a restless night for him. He could not
seem to get in the right position on his bed. The only
position that seemed comfortable to him was on his
belly but that position brought the wrong sort of
thoughts, sensations and images into his mind and
body, especially his body. At one point he even found
himself pushing his pelvis rhythmically up and down
at the luxuriously yielding mattress, and this unde-
liberate action made it plain to Billy that his experience with Big Edna had weakened, temporarily, the

Spartan control which he prided himself on having over his healthy young urges. He turned at once on his back and began to say the Lord's Prayer. Usually when he had a touch of insomnia, he wouldn't get past the first few lines of the prayer before he started drifting into dreamland, but this night he got all the way through it and was as wakeful as before. Finally, he realized what he had on his mind. He had maybe put himself into a morally vulnerable situation by hiring a new girl who was not just a good-looker but a spectacular beauty. With this realization, he turned back onto his belly and seemed to go right to sleep.

When the new girl showed up for work the following morning, Billy was very careful to show her no special attention, no sign of favoritism. He put her right to work as if she'd been employed at the drive-in as long as the other two girls. Of course he kept an eye on her without letting her see it. He had to see how quickly she would catch on, and it was amazing how quickly she did. You'd think she'd been a carhop at a drive-in since her first day out of a crib or playpen, she moved around so briskly in response to orders. She kept her eyes and her mind on her work and showed absolutely no sign of any kind of emotional instability whatsoever.

By midafternoon, Billy was convinced that this new girl, Gladys, was one out of a million, at a conservative estimate. She was not only taking orders briskly and cheerily, but she was shouting the orders to the colored man in the kitchen with an authority of tone in her voice that made the orders come out double quick, quicker than they would come out when shouted by Billy himself.

My God, she is a goddess!

That's what he said to himself about this new girl at the drive-in, and now that she had so brilliantly proven herself as the best imaginable drive-in employee, Billy felt free to express his pleasure with her.

Goddess, he would say to her, how are things going? Are they wearing you down?

And she would smile and say, No, sir, I feel fine, just fine!

Fine? he would say.

And she would say, Yes, sir, fine.

It was the sort of a conversation that has no purpose except to express good will. And Billy felt that good will was the keystone of their relations. Oddly enough, he did not feel uncomfortable over the beauty of the new girl. Perhaps his experience with Big Edna had purified him. It had been like an eruption and perhaps a great deal of violence in him had found a way out and left him a whole lot quieter and cleaner inside. He felt as though he had taken a purgative, one that removed all the waste matter in the body and left it sweet and clean as a newborn baby's.

How are things going for you, honey? he would ask the new girl every time she went past him and she would say, Just fine, Mr. Spangler. I'm not tired a bit.

She had not yet put on the uniform of the drive-in. Big Edna's uniform did not fit her and it had been sent over to the tailor for alterations. It would be back at a quarter after five and then the new girl would change into it. Billy Spangler was anxious to see how the uniform would fit her and he imagined that it would look extremely good on her. Her shape was young and perfect and the way that she moved her body, sinuously and briskly, spoke of good health and clean living.

Promptly at five fifteen the uniform came back from the tailor shop and Billy said to the new girl, Gladys, your uniform has come, honey.

Oh, good, said Gladys. Her tone was very excited. You could tell that she regarded the uniform as a privilege and was eager to get into it, the way that a proud young soldier exults in putting on the uniform of his army. But something had gone wrong, either in the measurements or in the alterations, for when the new girl came out of the girls' lavatory there was a frown of dismay on her beautiful goddesslike face.

Oh, Mr. Spangler, she said, the pants are too tight on me! The top won't button!

What? said Billy in a tone of chagrin.

Look, she said to him.

Billy could see it was true. The pants had been made too narrow across the hips or the waist and the top button of the fly could not be fastened. The fly gaped open exposing the sheer pink undergarments of the girl with the flesh showing through it the color of a fresh young rose, and all at once Billy was intensely embarrassed.

Shall I take them back off? asked the girl. Billy thought for a moment with his face to the window, gazing distractedly out and his hands in his pockets while he stood there reflecting.

No, he said, finally. Just leave them on for the present and tomorrow we can have them adjusted again or maybe even buy you a brand-new pair.

From then on Billy was acutely uncomfortable in the drive-in, and his discomfort seemed to affect the three girls. One thing went wrong after another, little things not worth mentioning, really, but the accumulated annoyance and strain was very heavy indeed by the time the drive-in closed up.

The new girl bore herself with irreproachable dignity. Billy had to give her credit for that. Even when another button popped off the gaping fly she did not lose her poise. I lost another button, was all that she said. She had already fastened a clean blue dish towel about her waist like a sash to cover the exposed pink drawers.

For a couple of hours before closing time Billy had been saying to himself, I better send her home first. But somehow it slipped his mind and when it came time to close up he was startled to discover that he had dismissed the other two girls and had told the new one to stay.

Well, he said to himself, I guess that I felt she needed a little more briefing on how things are done around here.

It may be that a touch of paranoia is necessary to individual felicity in this world. A man does not necessarily have to have a messianic complex but on the other hand, little good is derived from a continually and totally iconoclastic point of view in regard to himself and his relative position. Gewinner was a romantic. We have already found that out about him. The mere fact of his ascent to the tower of the Pearce residence offered us more than a clue to this dominant trait of his character. Of course, America, and particularly the Southern states, is the embodiment of an originally romantic gesture. It was discovered and established by the eternal Don Quixote in the human flux. Then, of course, the businessmen took over and Don Quixote was an exile at home: at least he became one when the frontiers had been exhausted. But exile does not extinguish his lambent spirit. His castles are immaterial and his ways are endless and you do not have to look into many American eyes to suddenly meet somewhere the beautiful grave lunacy of his gaze or to observe his hands making some constrained but limitless gesture, if only in the act of passing a salt shaker to an adjacent stranger in some nondescript beanery along Skid Row. He can talk to you with quiet wisdom about the ways of the world which he has traveled in his knightly quest. He can tell you where to get an excellent piece of nookie in a city two thousand miles removed from the place where you meet him or he can conduct you to one around the corner. Or perhaps his pocketknife has just carved a romantically large glory hole in the wooden partitions of the depot lavatory. He is not a good worker though he is sometimes brilliant. His jobs are not large enough for his knees and elbows and he detests the accumulation of fat on his body that comes with sedentary employment. He gets along badly with policemen. He is much too American for them. Our police force only gets along with false and dispirited people, broken upon the ancient wheel of Europe. Quixote de la Mancha has never been broken. The long skeleton of him is too elastic and springy. Our hope lies in the fact that our public instinctively loves him and that he makes an excellent politician. Our danger lies in the fact that he becomes impatient. But who can doubt, meeting him, returning the impulsive vigor of his handshake and meeting the lunatic honesty of his gaze, that he is the *one*, the *man*, the finally *elected*? And what does his madness matter?

America was built of paranoia by men who thought themselves superior to the common lot, who overlooked the ignominy of death, who observed the mysteries but did not feel belittled by them, who never paused to consider the vanity of their dreams and who consequently translated them into actions. So perpetually Quixote travels along his steep and windy roads, encumbered by rusty armor and mounted upon a steed whose ribs are as protuberant as his own. Behind him totters Sancho Panza bearing the overflow of knightly equipment and possibly a shade madder, by this time, than his ancient master. Sancho Panza has been elevated to knighthood in his heart and Quixote often dismounts in order that his equerry can rest in the saddle. Democracy has been taken in stride by Don Quixote and Sancho Panza as something forever implicit in the romantic heart, which is the true heart of man. Their language has changed. It is simplified. Now a syllable suffices where a sentence was necessary once. Sometimes they may go for days with only signs exchanged between them, the elevation of a single gaunt finger, slightly crooked at both joints, a cock of the head as it climbs into silhouette against a bank of gray cloud, the heavenward roll of the eyes, blue in the case of Quixote, dark brown in Sancho's. By silent agreement they will stop for the night, and now it is not unusual for both heads to rest in the padded crook of the saddle nor for the weatherworn hands to intertwine in slumber. Distance and time have purified their manners. Their customs are private. Sometimes they may fall out. That, too, is romantic. But somehow the roads they take in different directions always manage to cross again somewhere, and at the next encounter they are bashful as girls and each one wishes to take the smaller share of the wretched fish or chop, ceremonially prepared in honor of the reunion. And what of their deaths? They meet beyond the grave. Each one observes that the other is older and thinner but neither is so unkind as to comment upon it even to himself, for love of this kind is also a lunatic thing. Birds know them and understand them better than men. Have you ever seen the skeleton of a bird? If you have, you will know how completely they are still flying. . . .

Gewinner was solitary nearly always, he gave no evidence of being a very warmhearted person and in all external respects he bore but little resemblance to Quixote. But in his vision was that alchemy of the romantic, that capacity for transmutation somewhere between a thing and the witness of it. The gods used to do that for us. Ceaselessly lamenting women were changed into arboreal shapes and fountains. Masterless hounds became a group of stars. The earth and the sky were full of metamorphosed beings. Behind all of this there must have been some truth. Perhaps it was actually the only truth. Things may be only what we change them into, now that we have taken over this former prerogative of the divine.

It may be remembered, if it isn't forgotten, that Violet once received a message by carrier pigeon from her school chum Gladys and that, on that occasion, she asked Gewinner if he would like to receive a message from Gladys dispatched in the same quaint manner. At that time Gewinner could not imagine what the message might be. More recently, a number of pigeons had delivered a corresponding number of messages to the two conspirators, Violet and Gewinner, in the Pearce castle, and Gewinner sometimes, and sometimes Violet, had sent the pigeons back with answers to their dispatcher, Gladys, who was now, it so happened, employed as a carhop at the Laughing Boy Drive-in. Gewinner had even learned to swallow the incoming messages and found them not distasteful. They came in several flavors, and the importance of the message was signified by the flavor. Messages of routine importance tasted like lemon sherbet while messages of special gravity had a licorice flavor.

Of course the important elements of these messages were not the flavors of the paper on which they were inscribed, but—to avoid a premature disclosure of what was developing among Gewinner and the two young ladies—it is possible to quote the contents of a single message only. This message from Gladys to Gewinner, delivered at dusk by a pigeon white as a dove, gave him this bit of pleasantly romantic advice, if advice you can call it.

Dear Pen Pal and Pigeon Fancier, went the message quotable at this point, it is advisable for me to remind you that the use of the term "knightly quest" instead of "nightly quest" is not just a verbal conceit but a thing of the highest significance in every part of creation, wherever a man in the prison of his body can remember his spirit. Sincerely, Gladys. Then there was a short postscript: Watch the white bird returning!

Gewinner watched the white bird returning, he saw it open its snowy wings but rising straight up without moving them as if it were caught in a sudden, sweeping updraft of wind, and it disappeared in the air as if it were changed to mist.

Only a day or so after she started working at the drive-in, Gladys had taken Billy aside and told him that she was engaged in counterespionage for The Project but that he must mention this fact to no one, including Braden Pearce.

Billy believed her. He was so enamored of Gladys that she could have told him she was God's mother and he would have believed her, but it did seem to Billy that her methods were lacking in the sort of subtlety that counterespionage seemed to call for. She was continually putting through long-distance calls on the public phone at the drive-in, and whenever she had a spare minute, she opened a brief case and pored over photostatic copies of blueprints. At least twice a week she was visited by a man with whiskers that had a false look about them and they talked together in a foreign tongue that sounded like no earthly language, and one evening Billy was startled to see this man with the whiskers remove from his pocket a live bird and give it to Gladys, along with cardboard tags, bits of wire and a little dog-eared book that Billy presumed was a code book. Such methods of counterespionage seemed much too obvious to Billy. They were outdated. That night, when he and Gladys were alone closing up the drive-in, he told her about these misgivings.

Gladys reassured him. We're using these obvious methods, she said, to disarm the enemy spies with the impression we're stupid. And you've got to make up your mind, Billy, whether you trust me or not. You've got to make up your mind about that now, right now, if you want me to go on operating here at the drive-in . . . or change to some other place.

This conference took place in the little office of the drive-in, and it suddenly turned into a very intimate thing between them when she switched off the office light.

Afterward Billy had a very proud and elated feeling. He felt that something big and wonderful was about to happen, and that he, in his own humble and ignorant way, was a partisan in it, chosen to be one.

Father Acheson of St. Mary's Cathedral and the Reverend Doctor Peters of the Methodist Episcopal Church had both been invited to dine at the Pearce residence on the night of Saturday, March 16. This was a sign of the new amity that had sprung up between the two rival pastors. Only a year ago Dr. Peters had been heard to say, I am going to break the Catholic stranglehold on this town, and Father Acheson had remarked that Protestantism and atheism were holding open the door to the wolves of Asia. The peacemaking had been brought about by none other than Braden Pearce who was to be their host at the Saturday-night dinner party at the Pearce mansion. Braden had taken a very bold step to bring about this new amity. He had sent each pastor a check for five thousand dollars, payable one month from the date of receipt, and with it a note saying, I want you two fellows to shake hands with each other on the speakers' platform at the next meeting of the Civic Good-Fellowship League, which is to be next Wednesday, and unless you do shake hands and pull together for the common cause of making this a one hundred percent Christian community, why, these two checks are going to be worth just as much as the paper they're written on when you go to cash them.

The device had worked like a charm. The two pastors had not only shaken hands on the speakers' platform but had thrown their arms about each others' necks with such a lavish show of fraternal feeling that there was not a dry eye in the house when they sat back down to the chicken à la king dinner.

Now they were coming together on a special occasion at the peacemaker's home. This occasion was the seventh anniversary of Braden's marriage to Violet. Only Braden's mother knew that this was the last anniversary of that event which would ever be celebrated. What happened that night was that Violet got really good and drunk for the first time since the marriage in spite of the fact that she had only one more than her usual number of cocktails. Mother Pearce had mixed them. A scene occurred at the dinner table. Father Acheson and Dr. Peters were dreadfully embarrassed. They had to pretend that they didn't notice a thing, though Violet was leaning forward so far that her string of pearls was dangling into her soup. Braden would now and then reach out and pinch her arm or pat her shoulders. She would sit up straight for a minute or two, but then she would slump forward again.

At last Mother Pearce rang a bell. Two uniformed attendants came in as though they had been planted right outside the door for Violet's apparent collapse to occur. They picked her up by her legs and shoulders and whisked her out of the dining room. Only Gewinner made any comment on the occurrence.

Violet seems to be tired. That was his comment. Then he rose from his seat at the table and said, Excuse me, please, I'll go check her condition.

Braden muttered something in the nature of a contemptuous vulgarity as Gewinner followed Violet and her assistants out of the room.

It was amazing how Mother Pearce acted as if nothing surprising or irregular had happened. She turned to Dr. Peters and started a conversation about the sad condition of her flower garden.

Last fall, she said, my chrysanthemums withered almost as soon as they bloomed and now my rhododendron and azaleas have turned their toes up to the daisies, but my daisies are as dead as my roses. Of course I know it's the fumes from The Project, and I realize of course that, after all, it's a small sacrifice for anyone to make for anything as big and important to all the world as The Project. Don't you think so, Dr. Peters?

Dr. Peters agreed with her completely. He said that he hadn't had a real bunch of flowers on his altar in such a long time he couldn't remember how long. Then Father Acheson chimed in.

Easter doesn't seem the same without lilies.

Braden had sat in irritable silence during this exchange of remarks about the flower situation. Now he spoke up strongly.

In my personal opinion, said Braden, it is time and past time for all people in this country, including civilians in no way connected directly or indirectly with government service, to stop thinking about their lilies and daisies and to start thinking about the many grave problems confronting the country all over the world today and getting no better tomorrow in my personal opinion.

Hear, hear, said Dr. Peters, and the other clergyman at the table said, Yes, indeed, while nodding his head in vigorous affirmation.

Braden continued his extemporaneous speech, expressing himself in such uninhibited language that Mother Pearce tried once or twice to catch his eye with an admonitory glance, the effect of which was so totally useless that her eloquent younger son went on expressing himself more forcefully than before.

Everyone knows, said Braden, that before we put Stew Hammersmith in the White House, that house was occupied by a long succession of fools, one fool after another, a continual daisy chain of pussyfooting old fools without a realistic idea of a progressive nature in the whole goddamn lot of them. They were just there sitting while the reds and the blacks and the yellows were pulling fantastic stunts right out from under our feet, but now, in my personal opinion, we've finally got us a crackerjack man up there who can think as realistic as me or you about the many grave problems confronting this country all over the world today and worse tomorrow. And I'm not say-

ing that as a personal opinion, although this crackerjack man is my personal buddy that flies his own
plane down here for consultations with me whenever
I give him a signal. No, I just happen to know that
we've finally got us a man with a head as well as a
butt in the White House that can play the big-time
game of political power as good or better than he can
play golf or shoot craps, and I'm not shitting you,
brother.

Interspersed with Braden's speech were a good
many idiomatic expressions which are censored out of
this transcription of it, since they were only put in to
emphasize his points. When he stopped for a moment
to take a look at his watch, Mother Pearce got in a
word or two.

Oh, son, she interjected, I'm glad you brought up
Stew because my incoming mail this morning included a wire from Mag saying that she and Babe were
flying down here with Stew when Stew flies down
here this weekend. I thought you'd like to know that
wonderful piece of news. Isn't that wonderful news?

Yeah, wonderful, good, but, Mama, I wish you'd
let me talk for a change. Will you let me talk for a
change?

Talk, son, said Mother Pearce, you go right on and
talk, but I just thought that you'd like to know that
Babe is expecting to do "Babe's Stomp" with you this
weekend and Babe and Mag will be in the castle with
us.

Wonderful, good, said Braden, and I'm also pleased

to know that General Olds and his staff are going to make the scene, too. I guess we all know I'm giving away no secret when I give you my personal opinion that that old war horse has lost his balls in confronting the moral obligations of this country all over the world, and I don't mean the balls in his golf bag. What I mean is, he's a goddamn pacifist fool that favors us reaching some understanding in Wah Sing Mink and Krek Cow Walla, but after this top-level conference this weekend at The Project, two and two is going to be added together and if old Olds don't know what they add up to, why, by my liver and lights, sitting here at this table, he'd better say four is the sum of two plus two unless he wants to admit that he never learned to count past three in his life.

Son, said Mother Pearce, I want to ask you two favors. Don't use excitable language and save out some time for some fun with the ladies while they're down here. I'm going to throw another terrific clambake at the Diamond Brite and an Indian chief is coming to wrestle an alligator but I know Babe won't take her eyes off the door till you come through it.

Yeah, she's a red-blooded girl, but right now let me get back to what I was saying.

What he was saying went on for another half-hour while the cherries jubilee and coffee were served and the finger bowls set in position around the table.

Mother Pearce got up first. She rose from her seat

with a graceful, sweeping movement and said to the gentlemen, Will you gentlemen excuse us?

She had apparently forgotten that Violet had already gone, which isn't a matter of much surprise since she had counted out Violet to begin with, and it surely caused her no grief that Gewinner had taken a fast count too. Now she swept out, a regal figure as she strode from the dining hall toward the library, where she would soon be served a little postprandial drink in the nature of brandy.

Violet, on her way out! Gewinner, on his way out!

That's what she thought to herself as she paraded as if before cheering throngs into the room of a thousand books never opened. It was generally a quiet room but this evening the glass doors onto the conservatory were open and at one end of the conservatory was a large aviary of parakeets and lovebirds and canaries, all of which were now in a state of excitement and making a great commotion. Mrs. Pearce supposed they had heard her approaching and were expressing their delight. She paid the birds two calls a day, one after breakfast and another before dinner, and she would sit with them for a while, talking baby talk and making kissing sounds at them. They always responded to her visits with much chatter and flurry but this evening, hearing her approach, they were downright delirious.

Yes, they do adore me, she remarked to herself. I'll go in there and pay them a little call to settle them down for the night. So she went on through the library into the conservatory. The first thing she noticed there was that the air was quite chilly—and no wonder, the glass doors onto the garden were wide open. Now who did that? she asked herself crossly as she went to close the doors, but before she could close them, wings flapped over her head and a pigeon flew out. What was that, a pigeon? she asked out loud, and to her surprise she was answered by Gewinner whose presence in the conservatory she hadn't noticed till then. He was standing among the tall ferns by the aviary.

Yes, that was a pigeon, Mother, he said, that was a carrier pigeon that delivered a message to me from a young lady named Gladys who works over at the drive-in. It seems she has something like what they call a happening planned for the evening and the pigeon brought me an invitation to it.

Well, why don't you go? urged his mother, secretly meaning why don't you go and stay gone. She was tired of the mocking nonsense that Gewinner talked to her, the few times he talked at all to her. She'd better get him off on his travels again, yes, at all costs. But what the devil was this? she exclaimed to herself, as Violet appeared in the library, looking as sober as if she'd never heard of a martin that wasn't a bird, and dressed as if for travel and carrying a flight bag.

Why, Violet, said Mother Pearce, are you going too?

94

Violet gave her only the slightest of glances, and spoke past her to Gewinner.

I took a couple of bennies, I'm all straightened out for the clambake.

Good, our invitations just came from the haw-haw drive-in. Everything's A-OK, and timed to the dot and the dash, so there's not a moment to lose.

What shit is this? thought Mother Pearce, almost out loud, but they'd gone rushing past her, out the open doors to the garden and the garage.

Well, I swan, perhaps they're eloping together, wouldn't that be something too good to believe!

Your brandy, madam.

Oh, thank you, Joseph, she replied to the butler's announcement, and then she added, Close the doors to the garden. Parakeets and lovebirds catch pneumonia and wake up dead overnight. Good night, birdies, sleep tight, she crooned to the aviary as she went to her brandy—that she would drink to the providential way that everything seemed to be going in the long sweet and mellow autumn of her existence.

At about the time that Violet and Gewinner left the Pearce mansion the Laughing Boy Drive-in received from The Project an order for a quart container of coffee and a dozen barbecue sandwiches, this order to be delivered by Billy himself and not just delivered to a guard at the gates but brought by Billy personally to the Golden Room in the administration building, an order so extraordinary that Billy tingled all over with elation, there being no way to explain it except as a giant step up in The Project world in reward for his dedication.

There was a problem, though. He had sent everyone home that evening but the new girl, Gladys; they were alone at the drive-in.

How fast can you knock out a dozen barbecue sandwiches? he asked her.

To his amazement, she smiled bewitchingly at him and said, They're ready already!

One more problem: no locomotion, no wheels. His car had stalled on his way to the drive-in that morning and was still on the critical list at the Always Jolly Garage.

In no time flat Gladys had the quart of famously good coffee ready in a container and the barbecued sandwiches, steaming hot, in a glazed paper package.

Gladys, you're incredible, said Billy. Now get me a taxi.

Oh, that's not necessary, said Gladys. Mrs. Braden Pearce has just driven up outside.

Sure enough, she had. And Billy was so excited and elated he hardly noticed that Gewinner was in the car too, and in the driver's seat.

Come on, let's go, Billy, no hard feelings, Gewinner called out.

This was the sort of appeal to simple good fellowship between two men that Billy never resisted.

Wonderful! Coming, he shouted. They fairly

jumped in the car and Billy hardly even noticed that Gladys had jumped in with him. What a carhop! She had her hand on his knee and the fingers were creeping up from there to a higher position. Gewinner gunned the car and off it sped toward The Project.

Just before they got there, Billy said to Gladys, Do you hear something ticking?

Gladys said, Ticking, ticking?

Gewinner said, The engine needs a checkup.

Violet said, Tomorrow.

And the hand of Gladys was making such intimate advances that Billy pushed it reluctantly away and said, Wait till we—

Here we are, said Gewinner. And yes they were, they had now arrived at the main gate of The Project and were being accosted by sentries and barking dogs.

Violet leaned over Gewinner and shouted, I'm Mrs. Braden Pearce, my husband is expecting us, let us in!

The sentries seemed distracted by some kind of electric signal going beep-beep, more and more emphatically, from various parts of the grounds. One of the sentries waved the car along, but Billy had scrambled out with the sandwiches and quart container of coffee and was allowed to proceed on his innocent mission as the car sped on with Gewinner, Violet and Gladys.

Billy was aware that something must be going mighty wrong in the grounds of The Project. The electronic sound had become one continual scream and lights had started flashing and changing in color as Billy advanced on his errand. The lights flashed yellow, then red, then a lurid purplish color that seemed to penetrate all the vacant spaces of the sky and the areas between the concrete buildings and fortifications. Now people were running around and shouting at each other so hysterically that Billy couldn't make out what they were shouting. But Billy had the temperament of the perfect soldier and he knew that all he had to do was to follow out his instructions, which were to come to the administration building of The Project with this quart container of drive-in coffee. This he was doing and this he would go on doing no matter what happened. Nothing would stop him, not if all hell broke loose . . . but it sure did look like something had gone really wrong at The Project. He thought maybe he might ask somebody, but nobody was moving at a slow enough pace to be asked a question, so Billy just went on with his errand. Then a silence fell . . . broken almost immediately by a great voice that sounded like a recording. The voice announced: Our system has detected the approach of—

That was all Billy heard of the announcement, for his attention was caught again by a sound of ticking, and since he was now alone, no one for several yards around him, he heard it much more clearly . . . and, for gosh sakes, it seemed to be coming from—

He opened the lid of the coffee container and reached his hand into the scalding brown liquid and drew out the metal cube that was now, obviously, the source of the ticking sound, and held the cube in front of his astonished baby-blue eyes for a second or two before—

Well, before it *went off,* and everything went off with it. . . .

Yes, everything went off with it except the getaway spaceship which fortunately rose from its pad just long enough before the big boom at The Project to be in weightless ozone by the time of that far-reaching event. The ship bearing Gewinner, Gladys and Violet was called the Ark of Space—a reassuring touch of romanticism—and its destination is still secret to its passengers three and may still be secret to them for a long time to come.

It doesn't matter. They're so far away now that their watches are timed by light-years. In weightless ozone the concern with time is steadily left behind. Sometimes Gewinner strays from the cabin to the pilots' compartment, which is occupied by three astronauts in the full glitter of youth. They are amused by Gewinner's visits. Stories are swapped back and forth between Gewinner and the radiant young navigator, stories about the knightly quest as both have known it in their different ways. Sometimes a flock of stars will go past like fireflies in a child's twilight, and for a moment or two the Ark of Space will be flooded with light that makes Gewinner smile and say, It's bedtime —meaning it's morning.

And once, and once only, the communication system picked up a rhapsodic music, something like what the Good Gray Poet of Paumanok must have had in mind when he shouted, "Thou Vast Rondure, Swimming in Space." This music was interrupted and silenced by a voice so mighty that it made the ship tremble. Gewinner, at that moment, was in the pilots' compartment, and still having little command of their language, he didn't know, couldn't guess, what the mighty voice was saying, so he inquired of his closest friend, the radiant young navigator, what was the message, what was the shouting about?

The navigator said, Oh, many things that don't concern you particularly, but one thing that does, you've at last and at least been cleared for landing with us—of course for a term of probation.

Ah, good, said Gewinner, to whom the possibility that he might not be accepted had never occurred.

But what, he asked, what about this?

He touched his white silk scarf which had made so many festivals of nights on the planet Earth, far behind them.

Will this be admitted with me?

Why certainly, yes, of course, the young navigator assured him. It will be accepted and highly valued as a historical item in our Museum of Sad Enchantments in Galaxies Drifting Away.

Gewinner was about to dispute this disposition of his scarf, when the junior pilot sprang up, smiling and stretching, and yelled out, Champagne! Celebration!

Then all laughed and sang and joked together and offered toast after toast to each other and to the felicity waiting for them when they eventually reach the spot marked X on the chart of time without end.

MAMA'S OLD STUCCO HOUSE

MAMA'S OLD STUCCO HOUSE

MR. Jimmy Krenning wandered into the noon blaze of the kitchen for his breakfast coffee just wearing the shorts he had slept in. He'd lost so much weight that summer that the shorts barely hung on his narrow hipbones and thin belly. At first the colored girl, Brinda, who had lately taken the place of her bedridden mother at the Krennings', had been offended as well as embarrassed by this way he had of walking around in front of her as if she were not a young girl and not even human, as if she were a dog in there waiting on him. She was a shy, pretty girl, brought up with more gentility than most white girls in the town of Macon, Georgia. At first she thought

he acted with this kind of impropriety around her because she was colored. That was when it offended her.
Now she'd come to understand that Mr. Jimmy
would have acted the same way with a white girl,
with anybody of any race or any age or upbringing—
he really and truly was so unconscious of being with
anybody when he entered the kitchen for his coffee
that it was a wonder he smiled or spoke when he entered. It was Mr. Jimmy's nights that made him be-
have that way. They left him as dazed as a survivor of
a plane crash in which everyone but Mr. Jimmy had
died, and now that she understood this, Brinda was
no longer offended, but she was still embarrassed. She
kept her eyes carefully away from him, but this was
hard to do because he sat on the edge of the kitchen
table, directly in the streak of noon blaze through the
door, drinking coffee out of the Silex instead of the
cup she'd put on the kitchen table.

She asked him if the coffee was hot enough for
him. It had been off the stove since she heard him get
out of bed half an hour ago. But Mr. Jimmy was so
inattentive this morning he thought she was making a
reference to the weather and said, God yes, this heat is
breaking my balls.

This was the kind of talk that Brinda's mother had
advised her to pretend not to hear. He don't mean
nothing by it, her mother had explained to her. He's
just acting smart or been drinking too much when he
talks that way, and the best way to stop it is to pretend you don't hear it. When I get back to the Krennings', I'll straighten that boy out.

Brinda's Mama still expected, or pretended to expect, to return to work at the Krennings', but Brinda knew that her Mama was on her deathbed. It was a strange thing that Brinda's Mama and Mr. Jimmy's Mama had both took mortally sick the same summer, Mr. Jimmy's with a paralytic stroke and Brinda's with chronic liver trouble which had now reached a stage where she wasn't likely to ever get back on her feet. Even so, Brinda's Mama was better off than Mr. Jimmy's, who lay up there in that big old brass bed of hers absolutely speechless and motionless so that nobody knew if she was conscious or not, and had been like that since the first week of June which was three months ago. Although Brinda's Mama didn't know that it was the end for herself, she knew it was the end for old Mrs. Krenning and she sorrowed for her, asking Brinda each evening if Mrs. Krenning had shown any sign of consciousness during the day. Sometimes there were little things to report, some days it seemed that Mrs. Krenning was more alive in her eyes than other days, and a few times she had seemed to be making an effort to speak. She had to be spoon-fed by Brinda or the nurse and some days she'd reject the spoon with her teeth and other days accept it and swallow about half what she was given before beginning to let the soft food spill out her sunken gray jaw.

Brinda also cooked for Mr. Jimmy, she prepared his lunch and dinner, but he rarely would eat. She told her Mama it was a waste of food and time to cook for him, but her Mama said she had to keep on preparing the meals anyway and set the dining-room table for him whether he came down to it or not when she rang the dinner bell for him. Now Brinda only made cold things, such as thin-sliced sandwiches which she could wrap in glazed paper and leave in the icebox for him. The icebox was packed full of Mr. Jimmy's un-eaten lunches and dinners, saucers and little bowls were stacked on top of each other, and then some mornings she would come in to find that during the night the big supply was suddenly cut down as if a gang of hungry guests had raided the icebox, and the kitchen table would be littered with remnants in dishes, and Brinda knew that that was exactly what had happened, that Mr. Jimmy had brought a crowd home the night before and they'd raided the icebox and devoured its store of meals for Mr. Jimmy that he had ignored. But Brinda no longer told her Mama how things were going at the Krennings' because one day her Mama had struggled out of bed and come over to the house to make an effort to straighten out Mr. Jimmy. But when she got there she was too weak and breathless to talk. All she could do was look at him and shake her head and shed tears and she couldn't get up the stairs to see Mrs. Krenning, so Mr. Jimmy had to support her out to his car and drive her back home. In the car she panted like an old dog and was only able to say, Oh, Mr. Jimmy, why are you doing like this?

So this morning Brinda waited outside long enough for Mr. Jimmy to finish his breakfast coffee. Some-

times after his coffee he would come blinking and
squinting out the back screen door and cross to his
"studio," a little whitewashed building with a skylight, which no one but he ever entered. Its walls had
no windows to peek in, but once when he drove into
town he'd left the door open, and Brinda went out to
close it and saw inside a scene of terrible violence as if
a storm, or a demon, had been caged in it, but now it
was very quiet, only a fly buzzed in it, as if the storm
or the demon that had smashed and turned everything over beneath the skylight's huge blue eye had
fallen exhausted or died. Brinda had considered going
in to try to straighten it up, but there was something
about the disorder, something unnatural about it, that
made it seem dangerous to enter, and so she just
closed the door and returned to the comforting business of making up beds in the house. In the house
there was always more than one bed to make up, not
counting Mrs. Krenning's. The old woman's bed was
made up by her night nurse and the soiled sheets put
in the hall for Brinda to wash. There had been five
night nurses for Mrs. Krenning since Brinda had
taken her Mama's place at the house, and each of
them had left with the same complaint, that the
nights in the house were too outrageous to cope with.
Now there was a male nurse taking care of the old
lady at night, a repulsively coarse young man, red-
headed, with arms as big as hams, covered with a fuzz
of white hair. Brinda was too scandalized by this
change to even speak of it to her Mama. She was

afraid to go upstairs at the Krennings' until the day nurse came on at eleven. Once, when she had to go up to rouse Mr. Jimmy for a long-distance telephone call from New York, the male nurse had blocked her way on the back stairs, crouching, grinning and sticking his tongue out at her. She said, Excuse me, please, and tried to duck past him, and he had reached up after her and snatched her back down with one arm, like a red ham come to life, while the hand of the other made rough, breathtaking grabs at her breasts and belly, so that she screamed and screamed till Mr. Jimmy and his guest for the night ran naked out of his bedroom and the nurse had to let her go, pretending that he was just kidding. He called Mr. Jimmy "Cookie" and Mrs. Krenning "Old Faithful," and filled the sickroom with candy-bar wrappings and empty pint bottles and books of colored comics, and ever since he had gone on duty at night Brinda felt she could see a look that was like an outcry of horror in the paralyzed woman's eyes when she would come up with her soft-boiled eggs in the mornings.

This morning it was the male nurse, not Jimmy, who stumbled out, blinking and squinting, onto the little porch off the kitchen. Hey, Snow White, he hollered, come in here, Cookie wants you!

Brinda had taken out some of Mrs. Krenning's washed bedclothes to dry in the yard and had deliberately stretched out, as long as she could, the process of hanging the heavy wet sheets on the clothesline to give the male nurse time to leave before she returned to the house, but he had hung around, this morning, a whole hour longer than usual when he came out to holler at her. Brinda returned to the kitchen to find that Mr. Jimmy was still sitting in there, although he had switched from coffee to whiskey and from the edge of the table to a kitchen chair.

Miss Brinda, he said, blinking and squinting at her as if at the noonday sun, that son-of-a-bitch night nurse says Mama's just gone. . . .

Brinda began to cry, automatically but sincerely, standing before Mr. Jimmy. He took her hand gently in his, and then, to her shame and dismay, Brinda moved a step forward and took his bare white shoulders into her arms, enfolded them like a lost child's in her dark honey-colored bare arms, and his head dropped down to her shoulder, rested on it lightly for a moment, and to her still greater dismay, Miss Brinda felt her hand seize the close-cropped back of his head and pull it tighter against her as if she wanted to bruise her shoulder with it. He let her do it for a moment or two, saying nothing, making no motion, before he pushed her gently away by his two hands on her waist, and said, Miss Brinda, you better go up and clean the room up a little before they come for Mama. . . .

Brinda waited at the foot of the back stairs till she was certain the male nurse wasn't up there, then she went up and entered old Mrs. Krenning's bedroom. One glance told her that the old lady was gone. She caught her breath and ran about the room making a quick collection of sticky candy-bar wrappings, pint bottles and chocolate-smeared comic books, the litter in which Mrs. Krenning had flown from the world, still speechless, unable to cry, and then Brinda ran back down to the kitchen. She found herself shouting orders at Mr. Jimmy.

Mr. Jimmy, go upstairs and take a cold shower and shave and put on some clean white clothes because your Mama has gone!

Mr. Jimmy grunted in a vague sort of agreement, drew a long breath and went back upstairs while Brinda phoned the white people's undertaker, whose name and number, at her mother's instruction, she had penciled on the back leaf of Mr. Jimmy's little black book of telephone numbers. From the upstairs she could hear Mr. Jimmy's voice on the downstairs phone, speaking very low and unexcitedly to someone about what had happened, and presently the front doorbell started ringing and various young friends of Mr. Jimmy's began coming into the house, all seeming sober and talking in unusually quiet voices. Brinda put on her simple, clean white hat and ran to her Mama's. She knew that her Mama would make another effort to get out of bed and come over, but it seemed justified, this time, by the occasion. She was right about it. Her Mama wept a little and then said, Help me get up, Brinda, I got to go over there and see that it's handled right.

This time she seemed much firmer, although the effort to rise was probably even greater. Brinda got a cab for her. Holding her Mama's waist she could feel how thin the old dying woman had gotten, skin and bones now, but she walked with a slow, steady stride to the cab and sat up very straight in it. Presently they arrived at the Krennings' big house of worn-out stucco, now full of the friends of Mr. Jimmy with only two or three older people who were, or had been at some time, close friends of old Mrs. Krenning's. The atmosphere in the house was appropriately subdued, shades drawn, and everyone looking politely sympathetic, not putting on a false show, but observing the conventional attitude toward a death. There were a good many young men from the local air base present, but they were being nice too, talking softly and acting with suitable decorum. They all had drinks in their hands, but they were all keeping sober, and when the undertaker's assistants carried old Mrs. Krenning downstairs and out of the house on a sheet-covered stretcher, they kept a perfect silence except for one sobbing girl, who had risen abruptly and clutched Mr. Jimmy's shoulders, enjoying her burst of emotion.

Mr. Jimmy's glaze of detachment fell off him the very moment the door closed behind the men removing his mother from the house.

Okay, she's gone! And now I'm going to tell about my Mama! She was hard as my fist!

Oh, Jimmy, the sobbing girl pleaded. He pushed her away and struck his fist on a little chair-side table so hard that his drink bounced off it.

She was harder than my fist on this table! And she
never let up on me once in my whole life, never! She
was hard as my fist, she was harder than my goddamn
fist on this table, and that's the truth about her. But
now she's gone from this house and she's not going to
come back to it, so the house is mine now. Well, she
owned me, she used to own me, like she owned this
house, and she was hard as my fist and she was tight
as my fist, she set on her goddamn money like an old
hen on a glass egg, she was tight and hard as my fist. I
just got away once, that's all, just once in my life did I
ever get away from her—an old faggot took me to
New York with him and got tired of me there and
told me to hit the street, and that's what I did, oh
brother!

You want to know something? Even after I came
back to this place, I never got a key to it, I never had
my own door key. Not until after her stroke did I
even have my own door key!

She'd lock up the house after supper, and if I'd
gone out, she'd sit here waiting for me in this here
chair. And you know what gave her the stroke? One
night I came home and saw her through a front window sitting here waiting for me, to let me in when I
rung the friggin' front doorbell, but I didn't ring it, I
didn't knock or call, I just kicked the goddamn door
in. I kicked it in and she let out with a cry like a pig
being slaughtered. And when I entered, when I come
in the kicked-open door, she was lyin' here paralyzed
on this here livin'-room floor, and never spoke or

moved since, that was the way the old woman got her stroke. Well now, look here! Look at what I'm keepin' now in my pocket. See? Ev'ry goddamn key to Mama's old stucco house!

He took out of his pants pocket and raised up and jangled a big bunch of keys on a brass ring ornamented by a pair of red dice.

Then a soft voice stopped him by calling, Mr. Jimmy!

It was Brinda's Mama, in the shadowy next room. He nodded slightly, his outburst over as suddenly as it burst out. He threw the keys in the air and caught them and thrust them back in his pocket and sank back down in a chair, all in one movement it seemed, and just at that moment, luckily no sooner, the minister and his wife arrived at the door and the former decorum fell back over the parlor as if it had only lifted to the ceiling and hung up there until the outburst was over and then had settled back down again undamaged.

Brinda was amazed by the strength of her Mama. It seemed to come back like a miracle to the old woman. She set to work in the kitchen preparing a large platter of thin-cut sandwiches, boiled two Silexes of coffee and emptied them into the big silver percolator, and set the dining-room table as nicely as if for a party, knowing where everything was that would make the best show, the best linen and silver, the five-branched candelabra and even a set of finger bowls and lace napkins.

115

Mr. Jimmy stayed in the parlor, though, and drank his liquor till late in the afternoon, ignoring the buffet lunch that Brinda's Mama set for condolence callers. Only the minister and a few other old ladies drifted into the living room and ate a little bit of it. Then sundown came, the company dispersed and Mr. Jimmy went out. Brinda's Mama lay down on a cot in the basement, her hand on the side that pained her but her face, which was only slightly darker than Brinda's, looking composed and solemn. Brinda sat with her awhile and they talked in a desultory fashion as the light faded through the small high windows in the basement walls.

The talk had run out completely and the light was all but gone when Mr. Jimmy was heard coming back in the house. Brinda's Mama had seemed to be dozing but now her dark eyes opened and she cleared her throat and, turning her head to Brinda still seated beside her, directed her to ask Mr. Jimmy to come downstairs for a minute so she could talk to him before they went back home.

Brinda delivered this message to Mr. Jimmy who said, in reply, Bring your Mama upstairs and I'll drive you all back in the car.

Brinda's Mama's strength had all gone again and it was a struggle getting her up from the basement. She sat down, panting, by the kitchen table while Mr. Jimmy took a shower upstairs. Several times her head jerked forward and Brinda caught at her to hold her in the chair. But when Mr. Jimmy came down, she summoned her force back again and rose from the chair. They rode through the town in silence, to the section for Negroes, and not till Mr. Jimmy was about to pull up at their door did Brinda's Mama speak to him. Then she said:

Mr. Jimmy, what in the name of the Lord has happened to you? What kind of life are you leading here nowadays!

He answered her gently: Well, y'know, I did no good in New York. . . .

That's the truth, said Brinda's Mama, with sad conviction. You just got mixed with bad people and caught their bad ways. . . . And how come you give up your painting?

Brinda was scared when her Mama asked that question because, soon after she'd taken her Mama's place at the Krennings', she'd said to Mr. Jimmy one morning, when she was giving him coffee, Mr. Jimmy, Mama keeps askin' me if you work in your studio after breakfast an' when I tell her you don't, it seems to upset her so much that now I tell her you do, but I hate to lie to Mama, 'cause I think she knows when I'm lyin'. . . .

That morning was the one time that Jimmy had been unkind to Brinda, not just unkind but violent. He had picked up a Silex of coffee and thrown it at the wall in the kitchen, and the kitchen wall was still brown-stained where the glass coffeepot had smashed on it. He had followed this action with a four-letter word, and then he had dropped his head in his shaking hands.

So Brinda expected something awful to happen at this moment, in response to her Mama's bold question, but all Mr. Jimmy did was to drive right through a red light at a street intersection.

Brinda's Mama said, You went through a stoplight, and Mr. Jimmy answered, Did I? Well, that's O.K. . . .

It was a fair distance from the Krennings' house to Brinda's and her Mama's, and a few blocks after Mr. Jimmy had driven through the stoplight, Mr. Jimmy slowed the car down again and the talk was continued.

Mr. Jimmy said, If I don't know, who knows?

Well, said Brinda's Mama, even if you quit workin', you can't do nothin', just nothin', you got to do somethin', don't you?

I do something, said Mr. Jimmy.

What do you do?

Well, about this time of evening, I drive out by the air base, I go a little bit past it, and then I turn around and drive back, and, here and there, along the road back into town, I pass young fliers thumbing a ride into town, and I pick out one to pick up, and I pick him up and we go to the house and we drink and discuss ourselves with each other and drink and, after a while, well, maybe we get to be friends or maybe we don't, and that's what I do now, you see. . . .

He slowed the car down toward the house, stopped it right in front of the walk to the porch, with a deep sighing intake of breath, and released the wheel and his head fell back as if his neck was broken.

Brinda's Mama sighed too, and her head not only fell back against the car cushion but lolled to the side a little. They were like two broken-necked people, and with the uncomprehending patience of a dog, Brinda just sat and waited for them both to revive.

Then, at last, Mr. Jimmy sighed again, with a long intake of breath, and lurched out of the car and came around to the back seat to open the door for them as if they were two white ladies.

He not only assisted Brinda's Mama out of the car, but he kept a tight hold on her up to the porch. Perhaps if he hadn't she would have fallen down, but Brinda could sense that it was something more than one person giving another a necessary physical support for a little distance, and when they had got up the front steps, Mr. Jimmy still stayed. He took in his breath very loudly again with the same sighing sound as he had done twice before, and there was a prolonged hesitation, which Brinda found awkward and tense, though it did not seem to bother either her Mama or Mr. Jimmy. It was like something they were used to, or had always expected. They stood there at the top of the steps to the porch, and it was uncertain whether they were going to part at this point or going to remain together for a while longer.

They seemed like a pair of people who had quarreled and come to an understanding, not because of any agreement between them, but because of a mutual recognition of a sad, inescapable thing that gave them a closeness even through disappointment in trying to settle their quarrel.

Brinda's Mama said, Mr. Jimmy, sit down with us a little, and he did.

Both of the two chairs on the front porch were rockers. Brinda sat on the steps. Mr. Jimmy rocked, but her Mama sat still in her chair.

After a little while Brinda's Mama said, Mr. Jimmy, what are you going to do now?

I make no plans, I just go along, go along.

How long you plan to do that?

Long as I can, till something stops me, I guess.

Brinda's Mama nodded and then was silent as if inwardly calculating the length of time that might take. The silence continued as long as it might have taken her to arrive at a conclusion to this problem, and then she got up and said, I am going to die now, as quietly as if she had only said she was going in the dark house. Mr. Jimmy stood up as if a white lady had risen and held the screen door open while she unlocked the wooden one.

Brinda started in after her, but her Mama blocked her way in.

You go stay at the Krennings', you go on back there tonight an' clean up that mess in the place and you two stay there together and you look after each other, and, Brinda, don't let them white boys interfere with you. When you hear them come in, go down to the basement and lock the basement door an' you stay down there till daylight, unless Mr. Jimmy calls for you, and if he calls for you, go up an' see what he wants.

Then she turned to Mr. Jimmy and said, I thought a white boy like you was born with a chance in the world!

She then shut the door and locked it. Brinda couldn't believe that her Mama had locked her out, but that's what she'd done. She would have stayed there senselessly waiting before that locked door, but Mr. Jimmy gently took hold of her arm and led her out to his car. He opened the back door for her as if she were a white lady. She got in the car and going home, to the Krennings', Mr. Jimmy serenely drove through the stoplights as if he were color-blind. He drove home straight and fast, and when they arrived at the Krennings' Brinda observed that a soft light was burning downstairs, in the downstairs hall, and it seemed to say something that no one had said all day in so many words, that God, like other people, has two kinds of hands, one hand with which to strike and another to soothe and caress with.

MAN BRING THIS UP ROAD

MAN BRING
THIS UP ROAD

Mrs. Flora Goforth had three Easter-egg-colored villas perched on a sea cliff a little north of Amalfi, and being one of those enormously wealthy old ladies who come to be known as art patrons, often only because they have served, now and then, as honorary sponsor or hostess at some of those social functions, balls or banquets which take place on the fashionable periphery of the art world, she was diligently sought after by that flock of young people who fly to Europe in summer with one large suitcase and a small one, a portable typewriter or a paintbox, and a book of traveler's checks that hardly amount to a hundred dollars by the time they have passed through Paris; and for this reason, because she was pursued and besieged by this flock of gifted, improvident young wanderers of summer, she had found it advisable not to improve the landward approaches to her siege on the Divina Costiera of Italy but to leave them as they were left by the hand of God, a mortal hazard to any creature less agile than a mountain goat.

However, Mrs. Goforth was now edging timorously into her seventies. Other rich old ladies of her acquaintance were popping off, here and there, with the jazzy rhythm of fireworks on the Fourth of July. She had to have bright young people around her at times, that summer, to forget those reports on mortality that kept appearing in the Paris *Herald Tribune* or cables from the States, so she would send out her motor launch now and again to pick up a select group of them from such nearby resorts as Capri or Positano, sometimes even from Naples.

But Jimmy Dobyne was not called for or recently invited by Mrs. Goforth; he reached her by the goat path up the landward approach to her domain that summer, and it was the gardener's boy, Giulio, who warned her of his arrival by handing her a thin volume that had the shocking word "Poems" on its cover, passing it to her through the crack of her bedroom door and stammering in his pidgin English: Man bring this up road!

For several days her great old sunflower head had been drooping on its stem with incipient boredom and so Mrs. Goforth thought twice before she knew what to do, and then she said, also in pidgin English: Bring man out on terrace so can see.

When Giulio had vanished she picked up her German field glasses and crouched at her bedroom window in the white villa to inspect the Trojan horse guest. Presently he appeared, a young man wearing only a pair of lederhosen and bearing slung from his shoulders in a rucksack all that he owned, including four more copies of that volume of verse which he had offered as a visiting card to his hoped-for hostess. Giulio led him out upon the terrace and then drew back and Jimmy Dobyne stood blinking anxiously in the fierce noonday sun, looking here and there for his hoped-for hostess but seeing only an aviary full of small bright-plumaged birds, a fishpool of colorful fish and a chattering monkey that was chained to a pillar and everywhere cascades of violent purplish-red bougainvillaea vines.

Mrs. Goforth? he called.

There was no response to his call except the loud chattering of the monkey chained to a corner post of the low balustrade that enclosed the terrace. Having not much to look at or consider, Jimmy looked at the monkey; its enchainment, he thought, could hardly be anything but a punitive measure. Near it was a bowl containing remnants of fruit but there was no water bowl and the length of the chain did not permit the monkey to get into shade. Not far from the reach of the chain was the fishpool and the monkey had stretched its chain as far toward the pool as it could, which was not far enough to reach it. Without any thought about it, just as a reflex, Jimmy scooped up some water from the pool in the food bowl and placed it within the monkey's reach on the terrace. The monkey sprang to the bowl and started drinking from it with such incontinent thirst that Jimmy laughed out loud.

Signor!

The gardener's boy had come back to the terrace. He jerked his head toward the far end of the terrace and said: Come!

He led Jimmy to a bedroom in the pink villa.

Jimmy Dobyne was at least temporarily "in." As soon as Giulio left him alone in his guest room in the pink villa, Jimmy flung himself, all dusty and sweaty as he was, on the bed and blinked up at the painted cupids on the celestial blue ceiling.

His fatigue was so great that it even eclipsed his hunger and within a minute or two he fell into a sleep that lasted all that day and the night that followed and half the day after that.

After her siesta the day of Jimmy's arrival, Mrs. Goforth went over to the pink villa to steal a look at her uninvited house guest. She found him still in his *lederhosen,* his rucksack on the floor beside the bed.

She opened the canvas bag and, like an experienced thief, she rooted thoroughly but quietly through it till she discovered what she was looking for, his passport, wrapped up in a bunch of washed but not ironed shirts. She checked the date of his birth. It was in Sep-

tember, 1922, which confirmed her impression that he
was a good bit older than he appeared. She said
"Hello" several times, tonelessly as a parrot, to test the
depth of his sleep, and, since he remained as dead
asleep as ever, she turned on a bedside lamp so she
could look at him better. She bent over him, brought
her nose within a few inches of his parted lips to see if
he smelled of liquor or tooth decay as young poets
sometimes do when they're not so young any more.
His breath was odorless, but Mrs. Goforth could see
that it was more than the fatigue of traveling by foot
in rough country that had cast a color on his lower
eyelids as if a bougainvillaea petal had been rubbed on
them.

Mrs. Goforth was not displeased, on the whole, by
her close inspection of her self-invited guest but she
made a telephone call to check on his past history and
present reputation.

There was a lady on Capri who had known Jimmy
well in his heyday, which was in the forties, and this
lady gave her some information about him. She told
her that he had been discovered at a ski lodge in Ne-
vada in 1940 by one of those ladies of Mrs. Goforth's
generation and social set who had "popped off" lately.
This lady had brought him to New York and made
him a shining star in the world of Connecticut and
Long Island weekends, of ballet balls and so forth.
He'd been the odd combination of ski instructor and
poet, and this lady who launched him had brought
out his book of poems through the sort of small pub-

lishing house called a vanity press. However, the book had created a sensation. He had been taken seriously as a poet, but after that the poems stopped for some reason. He'd coasted on his early celebrity all through the forties, but lately things had gone against him. It started with his "sleeping trick" a couple of summers ago. Mrs. Goforth naturally didn't understand what that was but her friend on Capri gave a vivid account of it. It seemed that he had worn out his welcome at a rich lady's villa on Capri, he had been asked to give up his room for another guest expected and had tried to avoid this eviction by playing this sleeping trick on his hostess. He had taken a large dose of sleeping tablets but had also left an early-morning call so that they'd find him early enough to revive him.

As soon as he was able to leave he was told to do so. It was after that that he started "constructing mobiles."

Oh, he's constructing mobiles?

That's what he's been doing since he dried up as a poet. You know what mobiles are?

Of course I know what they are!

Well, he constructed mobiles but they didn't move, he didn't construct them right, he made them too heavy or something and they just don't move.

He gave that up?

No, as far as I know, he's still constructing mobiles. Hasn't he got any with him?

Oh! Mrs. Goforth remembered some odd metal objects among the stuff in the rucksack.

What?

Yes, I believe he still is, I think he's brought some with him.

Is he still *there?*

Yes. Sleeping in the pink villa, for hours and hours, completely dead to the world there!

Well . . .

What?

Good luck with him, Flora. Watch out for the sleeping trick, though. . . .

As Jimmy Dobyne came up to the breakfast table on the terrace of the white villa the next morning, he said to Mrs. Goforth: I think you must be the kindest person I've ever known in my life!

Then I'm afraid you haven't known many kind people in your life, said his hostess.

She nodded slightly in a way that could be interpreted as a permission to sit at the table and Jimmy sat down.

Coffee?

Thank you, said Jimmy.

He was ravenously hungry, the hungriest he could remember ever being in a life that had contained more than one prolonged fast for secular reasons. He tried to look about for something to eat without appearing to take his eyes from his hostess, but there seemed to be nothing on the chaste white serving table but the silver urn and the china; there apparently wasn't even cream and sugar.

As if she read his mind or the almost panicky tightening of his stomach muscles, her smile turned brighter and she said: For breakfast I have nothing but black coffee. I find that anything solid takes the edge off my energies, and it's the time after breakfast when I do my best work.

He smiled back at her, thinking that in the next breath she'd surely say, But of course you order anything that you like. How about eggs and bacon, or would you like to begin with a honeydew melon?

But the long minute stretched even longer and the words that finally followed her ruminative look made no sense to him: Man bring this up road, huh?

What, Mrs. Goforth?

That's what the little boy said when he gave me your book. I haven't read it but I heard it talked about when it first came out.

You asked me to give you a copy last winter at the Ballet Ball, but you were never in when I called.

Well, well, that's how it goes. When did it first come out?

In 1946.

Hmm, a long time ago. How old are you?

He thought a moment and said rather softly, as if he were asking for confirmation of the statement: Thirty.

Thirty-four, she said promptly.

How do you know?

I took a look at your passport while you were having that record-smashing siesta.

132

He made an effort to look playfully reproachful. Why did you do that?

Because I've been plagued by imposters. I wanted to be sure that you were the true Jimmy Dobyne, since last summer I had the false Paul Bowles and the year before that I had the false Truman Capote and the false Eudora Welty, and as far as I know they're still down there in that little grass hut on the beach, where undesirables are transferred when the villas are over-crowded. I call it the Oubliette. Y'know what that is, don't you? An oubliette? It's a medieval institution that I think, personally, was discarded too soon. It was a dungeon where people were put for keeps, to be forgotten. So that's what I call my little grass house on the beach, I call it the Oubliette. From the French verb *oublier*—that means to forget. And I do really forget them. Maybe you think I'm joking but it's the truth. Y'see, I've been through a lot of unpleasant ex-periences with free-loaders and I have developed a sort of complex about it. I don't want to be taken, I can't stand to be made a patsy. Understand what I mean? This is nothing personal. You come with your book with a photograph of you on it which still looks like you, just, well, ten years younger, but still unmis-takably you. You're not the false Jimmy Dobyne, I'm sure about that.

Thank you, said Jimmy. He didn't know what else to say.

Of course some people have got an oubliette in their minds. That's also a good institution, a mental oubliette, but I am afflicted with perfect memory, almost total recall, as the psychologists call it. Faces, names, everything, everything, everything!—comes back to me . . .

She smiled at him so genially that he smiled back, although her rapid flow of speech made him flinch as if a pistol were aimed at him in the hand of a madman.

However, she went on, I don't keep up with the new personalities in the world of art. Of course you're not a new personality in it, you're almost a veteran, aren't you? I said a veteran, I didn't say a has-been. Ha ha, I didn't call you a has-been, I said a veteran, baby! Ho ho ho . . .

Jimmy increased his smile because she was laughing, but he knew that it had turned to a tortured grimace.

There was an involuntary lapse in his attention to what she was saying while he said to himself: Don't give up! The road goes on from here. He wasn't certain that he was sure of it, though. Between him and anything coming after there was Naples again, and yesterday—there was Naples. . . .

He had walked along the long, long row of hotels facing Santa Lucia, the bay, and in front of almost every hotel there had been sidewalk tables where he had encountered people he used to know well. And even when they didn't appear to see him, although he knew that they did, he had stopped and talked a bit with them, as charmingly as he knew how. Not one of them, no, not a single one, had asked him to sit down with them at their sidewalk table! *Frightening? my God, yes!* Something must be visible in his face that let them know he had crossed over a certain frontier of . . .

He didn't want to identify that frontier, to give it a name.

To his surprise, he was standing on his feet and shading his eyes to peer down at the beach. Oh, yes, I see it! he said.

What?

Your oubliette, I think it looks very attractive.

Well, she told him, it's not in use this summer.

Why is it out of use now? It seems like a perfect solution, Mrs. Goforth.

Well, she said, it's still on my property and some people hold me responsible for the ones that I put there. I don't want to know, I never let myself know, what happened to them. As far as I know, or want to, they're all washed out by the tide, all phonies and freeloaders and so forth that think I owe them a living! What do you do? You don't write poetry any more, that much I know, but what do you do now?

Oh, now? I construct mobiles.

Oh, you mean those metal things that you hang from a ceiling to turn around in the wind.

Yes, that's right, said Jimmy, they're poetry in metal. I've got one for you.

Her geniality vanished. Her straight look at him drifted away from his face.

135

I don't accept presents, she said, except from old friends at Christmas, and as for mobiles, no, baby! I wouldn't know what to do with them. I think it would get on my nerves to watch them turning. . . .

I'm sorry, he said, I wanted to give one to you.

What's wrong with you? she asked him with sudden sharpness.

Wrong? With me?

Yes, there's something wrong with you. What are you worried about?

I'm disappointed that you don't want a mobile.

I don't want or need anything at all in the world!

She made this pronouncement with such force that Jimmy felt compelled to try to disguise his fright with a smile that he knew was no more a smile than the response to a dentist's order to "Open wide."

You've got good teeth. Young man, you're blessed with a very fine set of teeth, said Mrs. Goforth.

She leaned toward him a little, squinting, and then said: Are they real?

Oh yes, said Jimmy, except for one molar back here.

Well, I have good teeth, too. In fact my teeth are so good people think they are false. But look!

She took her large incisors between her thumb and forefinger to demonstrate the firmness of their attachment. See, not even a bridge, and I'll be seventy-two years old in October. In my whole mouth I've had exactly three fillings, which are still there. You see them?

136

She pulled back her jowls, dropping her lower jaw till the morning sun lit three bits of gold in the purplish cavern.

This tooth here, she continued, was slightly chipped when my daughter's third baby hit me in the mouth with the butt of a water pistol at Murray Bay, Canada. I told my daughter that child would grow into a monster and it sure as hell did—

Might I have some sugar? Jimmy interposed gently.

Oh, no, thank you, she muttered rather crossly, I never take it because they once found a small trace of sugar in my urine. . . .

A slightly frightened look clouded her gaze for a moment. All at once she sneezed. The sneeze was not at all violent but it seemed to throw her into a regular frenzy.

Angelina, Angelina! she bellowed. *Subito, subito,* Kleenex!

She sat crouched over, awaiting another sneeze, but all that happened was a couple of sniffs. She sat up slowly and fixed her angry glare on his face again. I'm allergic to something that grows around here. I haven't found out what it is, but when I do—

The sentence was no less forceful for remaining unfinished.

I hope it is not the bougainvillaea vines, said Jimmy. I have never seen such wonderful bougainvillaea vines in my life, or so many of them, either!

No, it isn't the bougainvillaea, she said in her warning whisper, but I'm having an allergy specialist flown down here from Paris to check me with every god-damned plant on the place, and every animal, too!

She brooded a moment more, her slow gaze wandering among the two cocker spaniels, the aviary, the chained monkey, a kitten gazing Narcissus-like into the fishpool. That's right, she growled. He's going to check me with every plant and animal on the place. . . . Then she got up and left him sitting there, as if she were blown from her chair by her third faint sneeze. She went, crouched over, halfway down the terrace on little tottering steps, then stood stock-still and sneezed for a fourth time.

What a shame! called Jimmy. Can I do something?

Her answer was incoherent or inaudible or both and a moment or two later she was gone from the terrace.

Angelina burst out of the white villa with a box of Kleenex, the excited butler screaming: *Giù, giù, giù!* The maid said something in terror, mixed with fury, and started in several directions before the butler seized her by her long skinny elbows and shot her in the right one.

The sun on Jimmy was beginning to daze and blind him. He got up and moved into shadow.

On the small serving table he suddenly noticed a fine white napkin covering something that made a slight mound on a plate. With guilty haste he picked it up to look under it and felt like crying when he saw that it was only a heap of crested silver teaspoons.

He had turned and started slowly away from the painfully brilliant white table when Mrs. Goforth's voice, a little muffled by a bundle of disposable tissues held to her mouth and nostrils, called to him from the foot of the stairs to a lower terrace of the white villa: Come down here. We can talk in the library.

Jimmy had been about to vomit up his cup of black coffee. He held it down forcibly as he descended the stairs.

Mrs. Goforth was waiting on the lower terrace, and for the first time he observed her appearance and costume, being no longer distracted by the hope of a breakfast.

The upper part of her costume, a halter strap, seemed to be made of fish net dyed magenta with very wide interstices through which could be seen her terra cotta breasts, only the nipples being covered by little patches of magenta satin. This fish-net "bra" was tied behind her shoulders in a flirtatious bow knot with two long dangling tails. Her middle was bare and her Amazonian hips were confined by skin-tight shorts exactly the shade of the bougainvillaea blossoms that overhung all the walls of Tre Amanti.

Come into the library, do hurry up! she called from the end of the terrace, and he tried hard to walk briskly but it seemed to take him an endless amount of time and he thanked God that she turned away just

a second before he felt himself sway, so close to faint-
ing that he had to rest the palm of his hand for a moment against the white stucco wall, bringing it away
stained with the pink of bougainvillaea that dripped
everywhere.

The library seemed almost black as he felt his way
in it.

Cool, huh? she called to him.

Oh, yes, very. . . .

I love to move from a hot place to a cool place, she
continued. It's the great pleasure of summer. . . .

He still waited for the room to come clear, however
dimly, till she called him once more and then he
started forward. His vision was just beginning to re-
cover, when—

He seemed to trip over something, halfway across
the room, but afterward he was not sure if he had actually tripped over something or had stumbled in
terror.

Standing there all naked terra cotta in the deep
gloom, quite motionless for the moment he caught
sight of her, she seemed like one of those immense
fountain figures in plazas of far northern countries,
but travestied by a sculptor with evil wit.

I am, she said, a completely informal person. How
about you?

I—

What?

I—

What's the matter with you?

I—

Oh, for God's sake, she blustered, are you going to pretend you're shocked or something?

No, of—*course* not, but—

Silence followed, and continued.

She suddenly stooped to snatch up a small pink garment. The bus to Naples passes in half an hour, she snapped as she retreated behind a great table.

Mrs. Goforth?

Yes? What!

I—don't have a penny. . . .

Naturally not! But I pay for as far as Naples and never farther! Also I'd like you to know that I—

Mrs. Goforth!

What?

Don't say anything more.

He covered his face with his hands.

The man was sobbing, my God, yes, he was bawling like a child!

Mrs. Goforth came back around the table. Some other person seemed to move into her body and take possession of her and she went to the sobbing young man and took him somewhat gingerly in her arms and pressed his head somewhat carefully to her bosom, as if it might break against her like a bird's egg.

You made me angry, she murmured, when you made that sarcastic remark about kindness on the breakfast terrace.

Why do you think it was a sarcastic remark?

Because everybody who knows me knows that I am colder-hearted than the gods of old Egypt!

Why?

I have no choice.

Why?

I've never had any choice. . . .

Give me a job, said Jimmy.

Doing what?

Proving that you are kinder than you think.

I know what you mean, she said.

I mean what I say, he pleaded.

Well, she murmured. Maybe if you stay here for dinner tonight—

I'd be delighted! he said, a little too quickly and loudly.

O. K., she murmured.

She had gotten back into her scanty garments. The interview was abruptly finished by the running approach of the maid, crying out before she came in: *Telefono!* Long deestance!

Then she threw the door open and Mrs. Goforth swept past her, marching out, and Jimmy said to the maid: Please bring some bread and cheese to my room, I'm in the pink villa.

The maid's face showed no comprehension but it was at least an hour later, in his room in the pink villa, that he despaired of his request being honored.

At five o'clock the bedside phone tinkled and he lifted it to his ear and heard Mrs. Goforth saying all in one breath, My friend is coming back with a very large party, I'm very much afraid that every bed will be taken for the next week or two, it's such a pity, we would have loved to keep you!

It was the voice of a young girl and the click interrupted it so abruptly he thought he ought to call back —at least for a moment he wondered if he could. He held the white enameled receiver weakly in his hand for a minute before it sank into him that he must move on again even though there was nowhere to move on to.

He rang the little electric bell by the bed but no one came, so after a while, giving up finally the idea of getting a bite to eat before his departure, he picked up his packed rucksack and went out of the pink villa into the sun, which was as hot and yellow as it had been at "breakfast," perhaps even hotter and yellower, and started back down the same almost impassably steep path by which he had come.

In the white villa the gardener's boy delivered a message to the chatelaine of Tre Amanti.

Man gone back down road.

Oh good, I hope so, she murmured, it being her habit or fate never quite to believe a piece of good news until her own observation had proved it true, and sometimes not even then.

THE KINGDOM OF EARTH

THE KINGDOM

OF EARTH

Talking about Salvation I think there's a great deal of truth in the statement that either you're saved or you ain't and the best thing to do is find out which and stick to it. What counts most is personal satisfaction, at least with most people, and God knows you'll never get that by straining and struggling for something which you are just not cut out for.

Now I passed through a period in my life in which I struggled. It grew out of all that talk which the Gallaway girl had spread through the county about me having a mother with part nigger blood. There wasn't a word of truth in it but as long as there is such a thing as jealousy in human nature, and that will be a long time, there are bound to be certain people who will give ears to slander. I was what is called a wood's colt. Daddy got me offen a woman with Cherokee blood in Alabama. I am one eight Cherokee and the rest is white. But the Gallaway girl had spread them rumors about me all through the county. People turned against me. Everyone acted suspicious. I went around by myself, having too much pride or character or something to try and force my company where I wasn't wanted. I was hurt bad by the way that the Gallaway girl had acted when we broke up. I was lonesome as a lost dog and didn't know which way to turn.

And then one evening while Gypsy Smith was preaching around this section, I dropped in there and heard this wonderful sermon on spiritual struggle. It started me thinking about the lustful body and how I ought to put up a struggle against it. And struggle I did for quite a while after that. The chances are it might of still been going on if Lot hadn't brought that woman back with him from Memphis which showed me just how useless the whole thing was, as far as I personally was concerned anyhow.

Lot come home from Memphis one Saturday morning last summer and brought this woman back with him. I was working out in the south field, spraying the damned army worms, when I seen the Chevy come turning in off the highway onto the drive. The car was yellow all over with dust and the spare tire was off. I guessed he had hocked it to pay for gas on the road.

I went to the house to meet them and Lot was drunk.

This is my wife, he said. Her name is Myrtle.

I didn't say a word to them. I just stood and looked her over. She had on a two-piece thing, the skirt part white and the top of it blue polka-dotted. It was made out of two big dotted bandannas which she had hitched together. It hung on crooked, and showed a part of her tits, the biggest that I ever seen on a young woman's body, sunburned the color of sorghum half-way down to her nipples and underneath that pure white and pearly-looking.

Well, she said, hello, Brother, and made like she would kiss me, but I turned away in disgust because I wanted her to know how I felt about it. It was a real bitch trick to marry a dying man which she must have known Lot was. Lot was a t.b. case and he had it so bad they let the air out of one of his lungs in Memphis. I guess she must have known what the setup was, that the place was Lot's and not mine although I did all the work on it. But Lot was a son by marriage and so, when Dad died, it was Lot that he left the place to. After Dad died and I learned how I had been fucked, I quit the place and went to Meridian to work in a stave mill there but I got these pitiful letters from Lot, saying please come back and I did with the understanding that when Lot died, which was bound to be pretty soon, the place would be mine.

Well, I thought to myself after meeting this woman, the sensible thing to do is just lay low and see how things work out, at least for a while. So I went back out to the field and continued my spraying. I didn't come in for supper. I told the nigger girl, Clara, to bring my supper out to me. She brung it out in a bucket, and after I ate it, I went to the Crossroads Inn to drink me some beer. Luther Peabody was there. He offered me to a liquor and while he was drinking he said to me, What's this I hear about Lot bringing home a wife. Who said wife, I asked him. Well, said Luther, that's what somebody told me, that Lot had brung home a woman about as big as a house. A house and Lot, said Scotty, who works at the bar, and all of them hollered. He's brung home a woman for practical nursing, I told them. And that was all that I had to say about it.

It must of been half past ten when I come back to the house. The lamp was on in the kitchen and she was in there heating up something or other on the stove. I didn't let on like I even noticed her presence. I walked right past her and on up to the attic. I pushed my cot in the gable to get the breeze but there wasn't a breath of it stirring.

I thought things over but didn't decide nothing yet. Along toward morning I started to hear some noise. I went downstairs barefooted. The bedroom door was open and they was in there panting like two hound-dogs.

I went outside and wandered around in the fields till it was sunup. I then went back to the house. The nigger was there to fix breakfast and after a while the woman came into the kitchen. She had on a light-blue satin kimono which she didn't bother to fasten around her even. The black girl, Clara, kept looking at me and giggling and when she set my plate down she said, What are you looking at? I said, Nothing much. And then she let out a laugh like a horse. I couldn't blame her. Me saying nothing much about them two huge knockers!

When breakfast was over I called Lot out on the porch for a little talk. Look here, I said, I overheard you last night in the room with that woman at half past five in the morning. How long do you think you'll last in your condition? Inside of a month that lovely Miss Myrtle of yourn'll fuck the last breath from your body and go on back to the Memphis cat-house you must of got her out of as fresh as a daisy!

That speech of mine made him sore and he acted like he was going to take a sock at me but I got mine in first. I knocked him off the back steps. Then she come out. She called me a dirty prick and lots of other nice things like that and then she started to crying. You don't understand, she bawled. I love him and he loves me. I laughed in her face. Last winter, I told her, he took the sheets himself. What do you mean? she asked me. Ask Lot, I told her, and then I walked off and left them to chew that over.

I went off laughing. The sun was up good, then, and hot as blazes. I had my jug of liquor stashed in a clump of snow-on-the-mountain. I went out to it and took a pretty good drink. It made me drunk right off because I had drunk a good deal the night before. The ground kept tilting up and down like a steamboat. I'd run a ways forward and then stagger back a little and laughing my head off at what I'd said to the woman. It was a hell of a thing to tell a woman. It wasn't exactly nice to tell anybody. But I was mad as blazes at what he'd done, come swaggering back with a whore he called his wife for no other reason than just to put on a show of independence.

I went back out to where I'd left the sprayer. The niggers was setting around it swapping stories. They got on up in a sort of half-hearted way. I said, Look here, if you all don't want to work, clear off the place. Otherwise hop to it! Well, they hopped. And by time to quit we had sprayed the whole north field from the road to the river. (You got to keep after them buggers or, Jesus, they sure will ruin you!)

When dark had come down I parked the sprayer under a big cottonwood and went back to the house. The lights was out so I turned on a lamp in the kitchen and warmed up supper. I had what was left of the greens and some corn and some sweet potatoes. There was some coffee left in a pot on the stove. I drunk it black, against my better judgment. It keeps me from sleeping in summer, especially when I am horny from not getting much and it had been six weeks since I'd laid a woman. I thought to myself, I am twenty-five and strong. I ought to quit fooling around and get me a girl to go steady with. The reason I hadn't till now was them false stories the Gallaway girl had started. The Gallaway girl was not in town this summer. She'd gone up North, knocked up and not by me neither, but not till after she'd spread them lies about me all through Two River County. The girl who worked at the hamburger joint on the highway told me she'd heard it but wouldn't say who from. I figured it must of been Lot that done the first talking. I called him on it. Of course, he swore that he never. I give him a licking within one inch of his life, because nobody else would have a reason to do it except he was jealous, and Lot was so fucking jealous he barely could breathe.

But never mind that, for that was all in the past.

The air in the kitchen was hot and it seemed to be humming. I guess my blood was kind of overheated. My hand fell down in my lap between my legs. My head was tired, and almost before I known what I was doing, I had it out and had started playing with it. I don't want that, I said. So I got up quick and went around to the big rain barrel out back and thrown water in my face and over my body. But the water only seemed to make it stiffer. It showed no signs of going back down neither. I put my two hands on it and jerked a little. It was a real big thing. Two hands just barely covered it. And so I set down there beside the rain barrel and jerked my peter. The moon was out and as white as a blond girl's head. I thought about Alice, but that didn't do much good, and jerking wasn't much fun so I quit and just set there and groaned and slapped at mosquitoes. There was no wind. There wasn't a breath of air stirring. I looked upstairs. The lamp was on in their bedroom. I listened awhile and I could hear them grunting. Yes, they was at it again. (I could hear them grunting together like a pair of pigs in a sty in a dusty place in the sun when the spring's getting warm.) I thought of her legs, just as soft as silk without a dark hair on them, and of her titties, the biggest that I ever seen on a young woman's body, the color of sorghum molasses halfway down and the rest pure white with little sweat beads on them. Then of her belly. Round and bulging out. And it would sure be good to press up against it or get her body turned over and up on the knees a little and then climb on and stick it up and under. Jesus, all the way in, right on up to the hilt, and then start working it in and out and feel it getting hotter until she started to pant and all of that hot, wet stuff come off between you. Good, good, good. The best thing in the world, that burning sensation and then the running over, the sweet relaxing and letting all of it go, shot off inside her, leaving you weak and satisfied completely and ready for sleep. Yes, there was nothing like it in all the world, nothing able to compare with it even. Just that thing and nothing more is perfect. The rest is shit. All of the rest is nothing hardly but shit. But that thing's good, and if you never had nothing else but that, no money, no property, no success in the world, and still had that, why, that would make it still worth living for you. Yes, you could come on home to a house with a tin roof on it in blazing heat and look for water and not find a drop to drink and look for food and not find a single crumb of it. But if on the bed you had you a naked woman, maybe not even terribly young and good-looking, and she looked up and said, I want it, Daddy. . . . why, then I say you got a square deal out of life and anybody that don't think so has just not fucked the right woman.

But that sort of thinking was doing me no good at all so I went back in the kitchen and filled and lit my pipe. I looked at the sink with the dishes piled up in it. A lot of improvement this Myrtle had made on the place. But then she wasn't a woman. A woman's a woman but a cunt is just a cunt, and that's what this Myrtle was, she was just a cheap piece of tail. I could use one, there wasn't no doubt about that. But if I brought one home to live with me, by God it would have to be one that I was able to feel a little respect for.

I went to the screen door to pee and waited several minutes before I could. A long way off I heard a hound-dog baying. It sounded sad. In spite of myself, I went right back to my old train of thoughts. I thought of the Gallaway girl and the nights we spent out there at Moon Lake, dancing and drinking and carrying on in a boathouse. She used to French me as well as everything else. If I had wanted to talk, I could of told people how she used to French me. No clean woman would do it. An old whore told me its what they call a snake-fuck, that tongue-wiggling business, but I've got to admit it sure feels good to have that thing done to you, and she was an expert.

Of course, I known it was doing no good whatsoever to run over all those memories in my mind, like shuffling through a worn-out deck of cards, but it just seemed like my mind was set on that subject and nothing would stop it. It's like the preacher says, the gates of the soul is got to close on the body and keep the body out or the body will break them down and overrun the soul and everything else decent in you. The fact of the matter is, though, I never did seem to have any gates to close. I was made without them. Some people are, I guess. Just made without them, and that was sure enough the case with me. I'd say to myself, This sort of thing is dirty, and I'd remember what the preacher had said and make a struggle to close the gates on the body. I'd reach for the gates to close them and find I hadn't a thing to catch hold of. I thought to myself, as I stood there on the steps, You freak of nature, you're letting in mosquitoes and not accomplishing anything but that. So I turned around and went back in the kitchen. One place was as hot as another. At least in there I had a chair to set on. So I seated myself in a chair at the kitchen table. I propped my feet up on the edge of the table. Between my legs that big old thing was throbbing. Yep, just burning and throbbing like a bee had stung it, and not a gate did I have to close against it.

I guess my trouble was partly a lack of schooling. I never think of anything much to do but drinking and screwing and trying my damnest to make something out of the place and not having much luck at it. I

156

guess if a fellow could pick up a book at night, that ought to make a good deal of difference with him. Oh, I could read, I could make out most of the words, but dogged if reading would close them gates on the body. I tried it awhile and then I would close the book and throw it down in disgust. Made-up stuff was not satisfying to me. They's not one word of truth in all this writing, I used to think, and the fellow that wrote it is trying to fool the public. So I'd come back to what I was struggling against. Poker, I like to play that but always seem to come out at the little end of the horn. I like to go in town and look at a movie or go to a carnival show, but only ever so often, not all the time the way some people do it. Looking at them screen stars don't close the gates on the body and don't ever think that it does. I've seen young boys that would play with themselves at the movies, and I don't blame them. They's nothing that makes a fellow quite so horny as setting there in the dark and looking up at one of them beautiful actresses messing around in a little pair of lace step-ins or a fancy wrapper. The screen industry is run by Jews with hot pants and that's why they put on all of these sexy pictures. You come back out and there ain't one inch of the soul that ain't overrun by the longings of the body.

Well, I was still in the kitchen while the night wore away, but I had a feeling that something was going to to happen before the night ended and I was not mistaken.

It must have been about half past twelve when all

of a sudden a big commotion begins. I heard him coughing and then her running and shouting my name in the hall.

I just set tight on the chair and waited to see what would happen.

After a while she come on down to the kitchen to fill up the water pitcher.

Didn't you hear me calling you, Chicken? she says.

I just set there and looked at her. The way she was dressed in only her silk underwear brought into my mind a thing somebody had wrote on the wall of a Memphis bus depot. Girls sure wear some real cute little French panties, and the fellow that wrote it must of been thinking of somebody built like Myrtle.

She filled up the water pitcher and clumped it down on the table.

Lot's took sick, she told me.

I didn't say nothing.

He seems to be awful sick. I wanted to call a doctor but he said no, he'd be all right in the morning.

I still didn't say a thing to her.

What's wrong with him? she asked me after a while.

He's got t.b., I told her.

She put on a shocked expression. How bad is it? she asked me.

I told her they'd let the air out of one of his lungs at the Memphis hospital because the X rays had showed it was all eaten up with disease.

Why didn't somebody tell me? she asked.

158

She set there and whimpered a little and I said nothing but just kept looking at her.

I've had a bad time, she told me. You don't understand how it is with a woman like me. I used to work in a dry-goods store in Biloxi.

What are you planning to give me, I said, your life story?

No, she said. I just wanted to tell you something. Then I was thin and I hadn't dyed my hair and I looked real pretty. I was fifteen then and I didn't go out with the boys. I was just as nice as any girl you could think of. But you can imagine what happened. The man that managed the store kept walking by me and every time that he did he would touch my body. First on my arm, he would just pinch my arm a little, and then on my shoulders and finally on my hips. I told my girl friend about it. Honey, she said, pretend like you don't notice, just try and ignore it and maybe he'll quit after while. But she didn't know Charlie. He pinched me harder and hung around me longer all the time. What could I do? Pretend like I didn't notice? I told my friend and she said, Honey, just take him aside and have a sincere conversation. Tell him that you're not used to that sort of treatment. So that's what I done. I went in his office to the back of the store. It was late one Saturday in the middle of summer. I said, Mr. Porter, I don't think you're playing exactly fair and square. What do you mean? he asked me. Well, I said, you seem to be taking advantage of the fact you're my boss to take some liberties with me which I don't like because of my decent up-bringing. But Charlie just grinned. He walked up to me and put his hands on my hips. Is this what you mean? he said. And then he kissed me. Then it was all over with me. I tried to walk one way and Charlie pushed me the other. He kicked the office door shut and backed me up against a big roller-top desk and took me by force right there. He had my cherry right there on that roller-top desk. He was a man about forty with sandy red hair. You know the sort that I mean, like a great big bull, and I fell in love with him. I got to admit that he made me happy that summer and my memories of it are still the best that I've got. They say that you always lose your heart with your cherry. I don't know about that. Some girls don't like it at first but I got to admit that from the beginning I loved it.

She wiped her eyes on the edge of the tablecloth.

Is that the end of the story? I asked her.

No, she said, the end was only beginning. He got tired of me. He said his wife had found us out and he had to let me go. Some girls would have made him trouble. I could of because I was only fifteen at the time. But I had too much pride so I just packed up and moved to Pensacola. Then to New Orleans. I finally come to Memphis. It wasn't till then I ever worked in a house and then it was only to pay for an operation I'd had to have.

I picked up Lot on a street. He looked like a kid. Sort of thin and pitiful-looking. It touched me the way that he laid on me like a baby. He seemed so lonesome, and it's the truth that I loved him. He slept in my arms just like a baby would and when we woke up he said would I come home with him and we'd be married. At first I laughed. It seemed ridiculous to me. But then I thought, Oh, well, as the fellow says, they's a hell of a lot more to it, this business of sex, than a couple of people jumping up and down on each other's eggs. So I said yes, and we set out the very next morning. . . .

Now what shall I do? she asked.

Do about what? I asked her.

You, she said. The minute I laid eyes on you, the first glance I look at that big powerful body, I said to myself, Oh, oh, your goose is cooked, Myrtle!

So what shall I do about it?

Well, I said, when somebody's goose is cooked the best way to have it is cooked with plenty of gravy.

I picked up the lamp off the table and started up the stairs. She followed behind me. At the door of Lot's room she stopped but I kept going on. I known she would follow. I went on up to the attic and dropped my clothes on the floor beside the cot and set down on it and waited for her to come up which I known she would do. I don't think I ever in all my life looked forward to anything so much as I did to that woman coming up to bed with me. Of course, I was horny and crazy to get my gun off, but it wasn't just that. It was partly the fact that she was Lot's wife and the place had gone to Lot and he was the son by

marriage and I was just a wood's colt that people ac-
cused of having some nigger blood. All that was
mixed up in it. But anyhow I had never in all my life
wanted anything so bad as I did for that woman to
come up and go to bed with me. It wasn't five minutes before I heard her footsteps on the stairs coming
up to the attic. And then I realized that I had been
praying. I had been setting there praying to God to
send that woman up to me. What do you make of
that? Why would God have answered a prayer like
that? What sort of God would pay attention to a
prayer like that coming from someone like me who is
sold to the Devil when thousands of good people's
prayers, such as prayers for the sick and suffering and
dying, are given no mind, no more than so many
crickets buzzing outdoors in the summer. It just goes
to show how little sense there is in all this religion
and all this talk of Salvation. One fool is as big as another on this earth and they're all big enough.

But that is beside the point now. The point is Lot's
wife was coming up to bed with me. And when I
heard her coming, it stood straight up so you could
hang a hat on it. I spread my legs and she came toward me and stooped beside the cot and stroked it
and kissed it like it was something holy. She giggled
and crooned and carried on something outlandish. I
just lay back and looked at the sky and enjoyed it. Finally she wiggled up and got on the cot beside me. I
felt of her body. So big and hot like a mountain that

THE KINGDOM OF EARTH

had a furnace inside it. I wanted to get inside that
wonderful mountain. I ripped the drawers off her bottom. She pushed it up off the cot. Then I climbed on.
She put the head of it in. I give a push and she yelled
out, God Almighty. I drew it back and gave it another
shove and she said, Oh, Blessed Mary. She said her
prayers, at least that's how it sounded, all of the time
that I was giving it to her. And when I come, and she
did at the same time, I swear that her yelling nearly
took the roof off. Oh, Blessed Mary, Mother of God,
she shouted. I had to laugh. I thought the roof would
blow off. And he must have heard her downstairs because it was just about that time that he started bawling our names.

Even before I come downstairs in the morning I
known Lot was dead. And sure enough he was. I
found his body laying across the doorsill. He'd gotten
down out of bed and crawled on the floor as far as the
door to the bedroom. He'd pushed the door half open.
His body was stretched out halfway over the sill, and
the blood that now was dried in the hot yellow sun-
light had made a stream, or what was a stream till it
dried, from the foot of the bed to the spot where his
head was resting. The bed was just like a hog had
been kilt on it. I wasn't surprised, because all of that
livelong night we'd heard him bawling out, Myrtle,
Myrtle, Myrtle. And later on he yelled my name out,
Chicken, Chicken, Chicken. And once or twice she
said in a half-hearted way, I reckon I better go down

163

and make him hush that Godforsaken bawling. But I said, No, the bawling is good for his lungs. So we kept right on having our fun in the attic. The bawling quit by and by, a little while after sunup, and then it was quiet and I thought to myself, Lot's dead.

I called to Myrtle and she come downstairs too. We stood together in front of the door and looked at him.

Poor little kid, said Myrtle. She started to cry. But not very much or for long.

It's all for the best, I told her, and after a while she said she guessed it was, too.

We got hitched up that winter. I think she had already made up her mind to do it but stalled around for a while, pretending she couldn't decide if she wanted to go on back to the sporting house in Memphis or stay on here. I made out like I didn't care much which she did, so she come around and said, Yes, I'll stay here.

So we two got hitched up on the first of December. We have our troubles but get on pretty good, as good as most young couples do in the country. We're expecting a baby about the end of the summer. If it's a boy we aim to call him Lot, in memory of my brother, and if it's a girl I guess we will call her Lottie.

And now it seems like everything in my life is straightened out. I don't ever worry about them spiritual gates the preacher said to keep shut. Not having no gates can save you a lot of trouble. And after all, what does anyone know about the Kingdom of Heaven? It's earth I'm after and now I am honest about it and don't pretend I'm nothing but what I am, a lustful creature determined on satisfaction and likely as not to get my full share of it.

"GRAND"

"GRAND"

MY grandmother formed quiet but deeply emotional attachments to places and people and would
have been happy to stay forever and ever in one rec-
tory, once her bedroom was papered in lemon yellow and the white curtains were hung there, once she
had acquired a few pupils in violin and piano, but
my grandfather always dreamed of movement and
change, a dream from which he has not yet wakened
in this ninety-sixth spring of his life.

Although he was married to a living poem, and
must have known it, my grandfather's sole complaints
against his wife were that she had no appreciation of
poetry and not much sense of humor. "When we were

quite young," he said, "I used to spend evenings reading poetry to her and she would fall asleep while I read"—which has sometimes made me wonder if her addiction to staying and his to going was the only difference which her infinite understanding had settled between them. My grandfather still is, and doubtless always has been, an unconsciously and childishly selfish man. He is humble and affectionate but incurably set upon satisfying his own impulses whatever they may be, and it was not until the last two or three years of their lives together that my grandmother began to rebel against it, and then it was for a reason that she couldn't tell him, the reason of death being in her, no longer possible to fly in front of but making it necessary, at last, to insist on staying when he wanted to leave.

When she married him she had not expected him to enter the ministry. He was then a schoolteacher and doing well at that vocation. He was a natural teacher, and soon after their marriage he was made head of a private girls' school in East Tennessee and my grandmother taught music there. At one time she had as many as fifty pupils in violin and piano. Their combined incomes made them quite well off for those days.

Then all at once he told her that he had made up his mind to enter the Church, and from that time till the end of her days my grandmother never again knew what it was to live without personal privation. During that interval the reverend and charmingly

selfish gentleman would conduct parties of Episcopalian ladies through Europe, deck himself out in the
finest clerical vestments from New York and London,
go summers to Chautauqua and take courses at Se-
wanee, while my grandmother would lose teeth to
save dental expenses, choose her eyeglasses from a
counter at Woolworth's, wear at the age of sixty
dresses which were made over from relics of her
bridal trousseau, disguise illness to avoid the expense
of doctors. She took eighteen-hour trips sitting up in a
day coach whenever summertime or another crisis in
her daughter's household called her to St. Louis, did
all her own housework and laundry, sometimes kept
two or three roomers, taught violin, taught piano,
made dresses for my mother when my mother was a
young lady, and afterwards for my sister, took an ac-
tive part in all the women's guilds and auxiliaries, listened patiently and silently through fifty-five years of
Southern Episcopalian ladies' guff and gossip, smiled
beautifully but not widely in order not to show miss-
ing teeth, spoke softly, sometimes laughed like a shy
girl although my grandfather often said that she
wouldn't know a joke if she bumped into one in the
middle of the road, skimped all year long—doing all
these things without the aid of a servant, so that once
a year, in the summer, she could take the long day-
coach trip to St. Louis to visit her only child, my
mother, and her three grandchildren which included
myself and my sister and our little brother. She always came with a remarkable sum of money sewed up

in her corset. I don't know just how much, but probably several hundred dollars—in spite of the fact that my grandfather's salary as a minister never exceeded a hundred and fifty dollars a month.

We called her "Grand." Her coming meant nickels for ice cream, quarters for movies, picnics in Forest Park. It meant soft and gay laughter like the laughter of girls between our mother and her mother, voices that ran up and down like finger exercises on the piano. It meant a return of grace from exile in the South and it meant the propitiation of my desperate father's wrath at life and the world which he, unhappy man, could never help taking out upon his children—except when the presence, like music, of my grandmother in the furiously close little city apartment cast a curious unworldly spell of peace over all there confined.

And so it was through the years, almost without any change at all, as we grew older. "Grand" was all that we knew of God in our lives! Providence was money sewed in her corset!

My grandmother never really needed a corset and why she wore one I don't quite know. She was never anything but straight and slender, and she bore herself with the erect, simple pride of a queen or a peasant. Her family were German—her maiden name was Rosina Maria Francesca Otte. Her parents had emigrated to America from Hamburg, I suppose sometime in the first half of the past century. They were Lutherans but my grandmother was educated in a

Catholic convent and at the Cincinnati Conservatory
of Music. I never saw my grandmother's father but he
looks in pictures like Bismarck. I barely remember her
mother, in fact I only remember that she was a spry
little old lady who referred to scissors as "shears."
About my great-grandfather Otto I remember only
that it was said of him that he declined to eat salads
because he said that grass was only for cows, and that
he had come to America in order to avoid military
service. He made a large fortune as a merchant and
then he lost it all. The last bit of it was exchanged for
a farm in East Tennessee, and this farm had an almost
legendary character in my grandmother's life.

My grandmother Rose was one of four children
who scattered like blown leaves when the family fortune was gone. One of the two brothers disappeared
and was never heard of again, and the other, Clemence, still lives in Mobile, Alabama, and must be near
ninety. My grandmother had a sister named Estelle
who married twice, first to a Tennessee youth named
Preston Faller who died young and then to an older
man named Ralston, a judge who had the dubious dis-
tinction of presiding over the famous Scopes trial in
East Tennessee, which was known as the "Monkey
trial." Once or twice, in the summer, "Grand" took us
to South Pittsburgh, Tennessee, to visit "the Ral-
stons," about which I remember honey kept in a barrel on the back porch, hot sun on pine needles, and
the wildness and beauty of my grandmother's
nephew, young Preston Faller Jr., whistling as he

dressed for a dance in a room that contains in my memory only a glittering brass bed and roses on the wallpaper and dusk turning violet at the open windows. But I was a child of seven and it is really only the honey in the barrel on the back porch that I remember very clearly, and the watermelons set to cool in the spring water and the well water that tasted of iron, and the mornings being such mornings! I do remember that Preston Faller Jr. would drive his stepfather's car without permission to other towns and stay nights and I remember that once he took me to a minstrel show and that there was an accordion played in this show, and that the keys or buttons of the accordion are remembered as diamonds and emeralds and rubies set in mother-of-pearl. Preston Faller Jr. now lives in Seattle and is doing well there and has sent us pictures of his house and his Cadillac car. And to think that he was such a ne'er-do-well boy! But he was the son of the sister of my grandmother—how time flies!—he's over fifty now. . . .

I spoke a while back of my grandmother's inherited farm which her bankrupt parents had retired to in East Tennessee. Actually it was only about two hundred acres of rocky, hilly soil—well, maybe three or four hundred acres—but it was divided by inheritance among the two sisters, my grandmother and Estelle, and their only known living brother, Clemence. Estelle died early of asthma and an overdose of morphine administered by a confused country doctor, and so this legendary farm belonged to my grandmother

and her brother and the children of her sister. It was
administered by Judge Ralston, the widower of Estelle. I remember only two things about it, or three.
One, that my great-aunt Estelle had to live on it prior
to her first marriage and that she told my grandmother that she was so lonely that she used to shout
hello on the front porch in order to hear an echo from
an opposite mountain. Then I remember that some of
the timber was sold for several hundred dollars and
that the proceeds were passed out among all the in-
heritors like holy wafers at Communion. And then I
remember, finally, that one time, probably after the
death of Judge Ralston, my grandmother paid a vale-
dictory visit to this farm, which she had always
dreamed might someday prove to contain a valuable
deposit of mineral or oil or something, and found that
the old homestead had been reduced to a single room
which contained an old female squatter. This ancient
squatter could not satisfactorily explain how she came
to be there on my grandmother's property. "We came
by and stayed" was about all she could say. My grandmother inquired what had become of the large porch
and the stone chimney and the other rooms and the
female squatter said that her husband and sons had
had to burn the logs for fire in winter, and that was
what had become of the porch and other rooms, that
they had disposed financially of the stones in the
chimney, too. My grandmother then inquired where
they were, these male members of the squatter household, and the finger-thin old lady informed her that

the husband had died and that the sons had gone in town a year ago with a big load of lumber and had never returned and she was still sitting there waiting for them to return or some word of them. . . .

That was the end of the story of the farm, which had meant to my grandmother an assurance against a future in which she thought maybe all of us might have need of a bit of land to retire to. . . .

The one thing that my grandmother dreaded most in the world was the spectre of that dependence which overtakes so many aged people at the end of their days, of having to be supported and cared for by relatives. In my grandmother's case there were no relatives who had ever stopped being at least emotionally dependent on her, but nevertheless this dread hung over her and that was why she continued to keep house in Memphis long after she was physically able to bear it and only gave up and came to St. Louis a few months before her death.

Some years earlier than that, when she and Grandfather were living in Memphis on his retirement pension of eighty-five dollars a month, I took refuge with them once more, after suffering a nervous collapse at my job in a St. Louis wholesale shoe company. As soon as I was able to travel, I took flight to their tiny cottage in Memphis and slept on the cot in the parlor. That summer I had a closer brush with lunacy than I had had any time since the shattering storms of my earliest adolescence, but gradually once again, as it had in those early crises, my grandmother's mysteriously peace-giving presence drew me back to at least a passable proximation of sanity. And when fall came I set out upon that long upward haul as a professional writer, that desperate, stumbling climb which brought me at last, exhausted but still breathing, out upon the supposedly sunny plateau of "fame and fortune." It began that Memphis summer of 1934. Also that summer, a turning point in my life, something of an opposite nature occurred to "Grand." Through the years, through her miracles of providence, her kitchen drudgery, her privations and music pupils and so forth, she had managed to save out of their tiny income enough to purchase what finally amounted to $7500 in government bonds.

One morning that memorable summer a pair of nameless con men came to call upon my fantastically unworldly grandfather. They talked to him for a while on the porch in excited undertones. He was already getting deaf, although he was then a relatively spry youth of eighty, and I saw him leaning toward them cupping an ear and giving quick nods of mysterious excitement. After a while they disappeared from the porch and he was gone from the house nearly all of that fierce yellow day. He came home in the evening, looking white and shaken, and said to my grandmother, "Rose, come out on the porch, I have something to tell you."

What he had to tell her was that for some unfathomable reason he had sold their bonds and transferred five thousand in cash to this pair of carrion birds who had called upon him that morning and addressed him as "Reverend" in voices of sinisterly purring witchery.

I see my grandmother now, looking off into dimming twilight space from a wicker chair on the porch in Memphis and saying only, *"Why,* Walter?"

She said, "Why, Walter," again and again, till finally he said, "Rose, don't question me any more because if you do, I will go away by myself and you'll never hear of me again!"

At that point she moved from the wicker chair to the porch swing and for a while I heard nothing, from my discreet position in the parlor, but the rasping voice of metal chain-links rubbed together as my grandmother swung gently back and forth and evening closed about them in their spent silence, which was, I felt without quite understanding, something that all their lives had been approaching, even half knowingly, a slow and terrible facing of something between them.

"Why, Walter?"

The following morning my grandfather was very busy and my grandmother was totally silent.

He went into the tiny attic of the bungalow and took out of a metal filing case a great, great, great pile of cardboard folders containing all his old sermons. He went into the back yard of the bungalow with this load, taking several trips, heaping all of the folders into the ashpit, and then he started a fire and fifty-five years of hand-written sermons went up in smoke. The blaze was incontinent. It rose far above the rim of the concrete incinerator, but what I most remember, more than that blaze, was the silent white blaze of my grandmother's face as she stood over the washtub, the stove, the kitchen table, performing the menial duties of the house and not once even glancing out of the window where the old gentleman, past eighty, was performing this auto-da-fé as an act of purification.

"Why, Walter?"

Nobody knows!

Nobody but my grandfather who has kept the secret into this his ninety-sixth spring on earth, and those rusty-feathered birds of prey who have gone wherever they came from—which I hope to be hell, and believe so . . .

I think the keenest regret of my life is one that doesn't concern myself, not even the failure of any work of mine nor the decline of creative energy that I am aware of lately. It is the fact that my grandmother died only a single year before the time when I could have given her some return for all she had given me, something material in partial recompense for that immeasurable gift of the spirit that she had so persistently and unsparingly of herself pressed into my hands when I came to her in need.

My grandfather likes to recall that she was born on All Souls' Day and that she died on the Feast of Epiphany, which is the sixth day of January.

The death occurred under merciless circumstances. Her health had been failing for the last five years till

finally the thing she had always dreaded came to pass.
She had to abandon and sell the home in Memphis
and accept the shelter of my father's house in St.
Louis because she was literally dying on her feet.
Somehow she got through the process of pulling up
stakes in Memphis, packing away possessions that had
accumulated through sixty years of housekeeping and
then that final eighteen-hour day-coach trip to St.
Louis. But soon as she arrived there, with a temperature of 104, she collapsed and had to go, for the first
time in her life, to a hospital. I was not anywhere near
home at this time, the fall of 1943. I was doing a stint
for a film studio in California. I got a letter from my
mother giving me this news, that my grandmother
was fatally ill with a malignant condition of long
standing which had now affected her liver and lungs
and placed a very brief limit to her remnant of life.

"Your grandmother," she wrote me, "has dropped
down to eighty pounds but she won't give up. It's im-
possible to make her stay in bed. She insists on help-
ing with the housework and this morning she did a
week's laundry!"

I came home. It was a week before Christmas and
there was a holly wreath on the door and somebody's
next-door radio was singing "White Christmas" as I
lugged my two suitcases up the front walk. I stopped
halfway to the door. Through the frothy white curtains at the parlor windows I saw my grandmother
moving alone through the lighted parlor like a stalking crane, so straight and tall for an old lady and so
unbelievably thin!

It was a while before I could raise the brass knocker from which the Christmas wreath was suspended. I waited and prayed that some other member of the family, even my father, would become visible through those white gauze curtains, but no other figure but the slowly stalking figure of my grandmother, who seemed to be moving about quite aimlessly to a soundless and terribly slow march tune, a ghostly brass band that was playing a death march, came into view!

The family, I learned later, had gone out to that monthly business banquet of my father's world called the Progress Club.

My grandfather was in bed. "Grand" was waiting up alone to receive me at whatever hour—I had not wired precisely when—I might appear at the family door for this last homecoming of mine that she would take part in.

As my grandmother drew the door open in response to my knock, I remember how she laughed like a shy girl, a girl caught sentimentalizing over something like a sweetheart's photograph, and cried out, in her young voice, "Oh, Tom, oh, Tom!" And as I embraced her, I felt with terror almost nothing but the material of her dress and her own arms burning with fever through that cloth.

She died about two weeks later, after a spurious, totally self-willed period of seeming recuperation.

I left the house right after dinner that evening. She had washed the dishes, refusing my mother's assistance or my grandfather's or mine, and was at the piano playing Chopin when I went out the door.

When I returned only two or three hours later, the whole two-story house which we now occupied was filled with the sound of her last struggle for breath.

On the stairs was a stranger who had heard me knock before I discovered that I did have the key.

He said, with no expression, "Your mother wants you upstairs."

I went upstairs. At the top of the steps, where my grandmother's hemorrhage had begun, was a pool of still fresh blood. There was a trail of dark wet blood into the bathroom and the toilet bowl still unflushed was deep crimson and there were clotted bits of voided lung tissue in the bowl and on the tiles of the bathroom floor. Later I learned that this incontinent giving up of her lifeblood had occurred almost immediately after I had left the house, three hours ago, and still in her bedroom my grandmother was continuing, fiercely, wildly, unyieldingly, her battle with death, which had already won that battle halfway up the stairs. . . .

I didn't dare enter the room where the terrible struggle was going on. I stood across the hall in the dark room which had been my brother's before he entered the army. I stood in the dark room, possibly praying, possibly only sobbing, possibly only listening, I don't know which, and across the hall I heard my mother's voice saying over and over again, "Mother, what is it, Mother, what is it, what are you trying to tell me?"

I only dared to look in. My mother was crouched

182

over the figure of my grandmother on the bed, mercifully obscuring her from me. My grandfather was kneeling in prayer beside his armchair. The doctor was hovering helplessly over all three with a hypodermic needle and a bowl of steaming water and this or that bit of useless paraphernalia.

Then all at once the terrible noise was still.

I went into the room.

My mother was gently closing my grandmother's jaws and eyes.

Some hours later neighbors began to arrive. My grandfather went downstairs to let them in, and standing at the top of the stairs, I heard him say to them, "My wife is very weak, she seems to be very weak now."

"Walter will never face the facts about things," was one of my grandmother's sayings about him.

Then a year or so ago my mother happened to tell me that she had finally found out what my grandmother was trying to tell her as she died, but hadn't the strength to. "Your grandmother kept pointing at the bureau, and later I found out that she had her corset in there with several hundred dollars sewed up in it!"